MW01205928

DOCTOR'S SECRET SANTA

TRINITY FALLS SWEET ROMANCE - BOOK 6

CLARA PINES

PINE NUT PRESS

Copyright © 2023 by Pine Nut Press

All rights reserved. This book or any portion thereof may not be reproduced or used in any manner whatsoever without the express written permission of the publisher except for the use of brief quotations in a book review.

Pine Nut Press

PO Box 506

Swarthmore, PA 19081

pinenutpress@gmail.com

Cover designed by The Book Brander

1

DAISY

D aisy Mullen clutched the wheel of her father's old pick-up truck. The seat was pushed back farther than usual, to allow space for the roundness of her belly. She was sore and tired, but determined to keep a positive attitude.

The drive to Trinity Falls had been longer than expected, which she was sure had nothing at all to do with the twenty or so unscheduled bathroom stops. Now it was dark, and a haze of snow flurries shimmered in streetlamps and landed on the roofs of houses that looked like they belonged in a different time. It definitely wasn't like what she was used to.

Even the trees seemed too big. They met over the road, forming a sort of tunnel of bare branches that were being slowly frosted with snow.

Daisy didn't love driving under normal conditions, but driving on unfamiliar roads in the snow definitely had her white-knuckled. And in her condition, and after all that had happened, she couldn't help anticipating danger at every turn.

The Christmas music playing on the old car radio, usually her favorite, did nothing to soothe her spirits.

The scent of the French fries she'd bought at a drive-through a couple of miles back made her stomach rumble. She'd been desperate for something to eat, but once the snow began to fall, she was too scared to divert her hand or her attention long enough for a single bite.

From the cupholder, her phone buzzed to let her know that she had reached her destination.

Daisy pulled over and looked around in disbelief.

Her dad had painted her a really good picture of how he remembered Dr. Wilkinson's home and office from his visit years ago. He had described it as a charming house, standing in the center of a picturesque block, looking much like the other houses, and not like an office at all.

But she was clearly at the hub of the tiny town, where two streets of shops met at the corner. Her directions had taken her to Trinity Falls, but not to the exact address.

Most of the shop lights were off, but the biggest one, with glassy walls and a sign that said *Trinity Falls Co-op Grocer,* was still brightly lit.

She pulled the truck over carefully, thankful that there weren't many cars around. She'd never had to parallel park back home. At least, she hadn't had to do it since she passed her driver's test a couple of years ago.

She resisted the urge to hop out like she normally would have, and instead lowered herself carefully to the ground, rubbing her lower back a little as she straightened up.

Her pregnancy was going very well, but Daisy had always been on the slender side. Now that she was getting bigger, it was hard to get used to her new shape. Lately, she found herself worrying that if she got any rounder, she might just tip right over.

"Okay, girl, you've got this," she whispered softly to herself as she mounted the steps.

The sign said it was a grocery store, but there was definitely some kind of restaurant in there, too.

Her stomach grumbled again.

"Hold on, peanut," she advised her belly and its occupant. "I think we'll find something good in here for you once I get us directions."

Surely, someone in this place would know where the doctor lived.

As if on cue, a sweet-looking young woman in a shop apron came over to greet Daisy as she walked in.

"Hi there," the woman said. "I'm Lucy. Can I help you find anything?"

"Actually, I was hoping you could do me a favor," Daisy confided.

The other young woman leaned in immediately, an expression of happy anticipation on her face.

Daisy had no idea why, but she had a gift with people. It was nothing she could put her finger on. Folks just felt comfortable with her the moment they met.

"Of course," Lucy said. "What is it?"

"I can't seem to find the doctor's office," Daisy said. "My directions wound me up right here, in front of the store. Do you happen to know where his office is?"

"Oh dear," Lucy said worriedly, her face going pale as she eyed Daisy's belly. "I can call the guys at the fire department, and they'll get you to the hospital in two shakes of a lamb's tail. The firehouse is right across the street."

"Did you say you need the fire department?" an older lady asked, stopping her cart beside them. "I'll just run right over—"

"Oh, no," Daisy said quickly. "No, you two are so sweet,

but I'm absolutely fine. The doctor was a friend of my dad's. I'm just stopping by."

"Oh, thank goodness," Lucy said, breathing a sigh of relief.

"Sorry for the false alarm," Daisy said.

"Honestly, it's good this happened," Lucy said, shaking her head. "It made me realize our First Aid kit could be better stocked for more unusual types of emergencies."

Daisy laughed, and Lucy joined her.

"You girls," the older lady said with a smile, shaking her head and pushing her cart up the next aisle.

"Well, you're in luck. The doc happens to be my brother, and his office is right on this street, not quite two blocks down," Lucy told her. "It'll be on your left—a wood frame house painted white with green shutters. There's a sign on the lawn, but you have to look for it. Otherwise, it just looks like a regular house."

The woman looked young to be Dr. Wilkinson's sister, but she knew a few families that had large age gaps among the siblings. And running into her as the first person she met in town seemed like a good omen.

"What a lovely coincidence," Daisy told her. "I'm just going to grab a few things here, and I'll head over."

"You don't have to buy anything," Lucy told her. "Unless you want to. And you're welcome to use the restroom. It's at the back of the store on the right."

"You are a godsend, Lucy," Daisy told her. "Thank you so much."

"All in a day's work," Lucy told her with a smile and a wink.

Daisy scurried off to the bathroom, deciding she should make time for a pit stop. After all, she was only a block and a half away from the Wilkinsons' place. Even if it started snowing harder, and she was too scared to drive, she could walk.

The ladies' room was clean and bright, and in spite of the day's long journey, if she squinted at the mirror a bit, she looked none the worse for wear.

Feeling refreshed, she headed out and ambled down what looked like a deli aisle, hoping to find a premade hoagie she could scarf down in the car since her fries were probably a congealed mess by now.

But everything here looked like health food. It was all covered in veggies and even those horrible, worm-like bean sprouts. Unappealing, and without a doubt expensive.

I'll just eat my cold fries, she told herself.

She did grab a cherry pie with a sticker on it saying it was from a local farm. Her dad had always told her it wasn't nice to show up empty-handed, and, given what was on offer at the grocery store, she had a feeling she'd be sorry if she gave away the box of TastyKakes she had stashed in the trunk.

She paid, and headed back out, sucking in a breath of the snowy air.

The little town was so pretty. She hadn't noticed before because she was rushed and worried, but now she could see that it looked like something out of a storybook.

Her boots crunched in the thin layer of snow on the sidewalks as she headed back to the truck.

Once she had hoisted herself in, she grabbed a handful of fries and ate them, moaning a little with satisfaction. Cold or not, they were delicious and salty, and they tamed her ravenous hunger just a little.

After one more handful, she started the truck and turned around, heading down the street to find the Wilkinsons' place.

Sure enough, there was a pretty white house with green shutters and a subtle sign out front, about a block and a half from the village center, just as Lucy had said.

She pulled over and parked out front, grabbed the pie, and gave herself a small pep talk.

He might not have met you before, but Daddy said he was a good man, and that means he won't turn you away, at least not tonight.

She scrambled up the walkway and knocked on the door, stepping back to wait, with the pie held in front of her like an offering.

She was just about to knock again, when the door swung open.

The man in the threshold was so different from what she had expected that Daisy just gaped at him like a fish for a minute.

A man who looked to be in his early thirties gazed down at her sternly, his ocean-blue eyes, framed by impossibly dark lashes. His equally dark hair was a little too long, and hung over his forehead. A plain white t-shirt clung to his muscular chest, and a pair of sweats hung almost sinfully low on his hips.

She cleared her throat and met his eyes again, feeling her cheeks burn. What in the world was she thinking? She was expecting, and a widow, for heaven's sake. She had enough challenges without her subconscious trying to give her unwanted man troubles.

A wave of guilt washed over her, sending her emotions tumbling in the opposite direction.

It's all just the pregnancy hormones, she told herself reassuringly. *And you're hungry. Just keep your eyes on his face, and stay positive.*

"Can I help you?" he asked.

His voice was hard as flint.

"Oh, good heavens, you probably think I'm selling something," she blurted out. "I'm so sorry to have disturbed you. I must have the wrong house. I was looking for the doctor."

"I'm the doctor," he said patiently.

"Dr. Wilkinson?" she heard herself ask, even though clearly this wasn't the man who had served in the military with her dad.

"Ah," the man said. "The Wilkinsons moved to the condos. I'm the new doctor. I'm partnering with him for now. Are you hurt?"

"No," she said, feeling anxious again. "I hate to ask, but could you call them for me? His old home number wasn't working. Now I understand why."

"Come on in," the new doctor said, his expression and tone softening. "We'll get ahold of them for you."

She followed him into a charming living room.

He indicated the sofa and then slid his phone out of his pocket, tapping on the tiny thing with his big hands.

She opted not to sit, figuring that that sofa looked soft enough that it would be hard to get up again. Judging the firmness of furniture had become a surprisingly useful skill as her pregnancy advanced.

"Hey, Frank," he said. "No, no, everything's fine. It's just that we got a visitor here, and she's looking for you... Didn't get her name... Okay, shall I put her on?"

He handed her the phone.

Daisy put it to her ear, praying that the old doctor would see fit to help her, even without seeing that she had brought him a pie.

"Frank here," a hearty masculine voice said.

"Hello, Dr. Wilkinson," Daisy said, feeling flustered.

"You don't know me, but I'm Daisy Mullen. You knew my dad—"

"Oh Lordy, you're Hal Mullen's girl," Dr. Wilkinson said. "I can't believe it. What are you doing in Trinity Falls?"

"It's kind of a long story," she told him. "But basically I'm, um, relocating. And I was hoping to chat with you about maybe coming to work for you. I have my LPN now."

"Isn't that wonderful?" Dr. Wilkinson said. "We'll have a talk about it in the morning, absolutely."

"I, uh, also had a really big favor to ask of you and Mrs. Wilkinson," Daisy said. "I tried to book a room at the inn, but I heard back when I was almost here that they're full tonight. I hate to ask, but is there any chance I could maybe stay at your place, just for the night? I'm quiet as a mouse and I'll be out bright and early."

"Oh, dear," Dr. Wilkinson said. "I'm so sorry, but Sadie and I are in a one-bedroom unit over at the condos. We're getting ready to retire, and this place is barely big enough for a bed and the suitcases we'll have when we're off traveling the world. But I'll bet Dr. Webb can spare his guest room over there at the house."

"No, no," she said immediately. "I'll be fine. You have a good night, and we'll talk tomorrow."

She hung up before he could press her to stay with a stranger.

"You need a place to stay for the night," the man who had to be Dr. Webb said. "We have a guest room. It's not a problem for you to stay here."

She glanced up at him, debating.

On the one hand, she didn't know this guy, and she had learned the hard way that her own nature could be too trusting.

On the other hand, he was a colleague of Dr. Wilkinson

—his partner, in fact. And if Dr. Wilkinson was a good man, he ought to be a good judge of character, too.

Plus, it was too cold to sleep in the truck.

"If I'm not putting you out," she said tentatively. "And if you think your wife would be okay with it."

"I don't have a wife," he said.

Well, shoot. Now what do I do?

She was just beginning to panic for real when a little boy scampered down the stairs and streaked across the room to his father's side.

"Who's *that*?" he demanded happily.

"Those aren't the manners we use," Dr. Webb said patiently, his stern expression softer when he spoke to the boy. "Why don't you say hello and ask her yourself?"

"Hello," the boy said. "I'm Benny and I'm seven. What's your name?"

"I'm Daisy," she told him with a smile.

"Daisy needs a place to stay because Miss Trudy's inn is all full," Dr. Webb told him.

"You could stay here," Benny said, his eyebrows practically leaping off his little face. "We have a special room for visitors, and my Aunt Lucy stayed there when my daddy had to go to a conference, and we made finger paintings together, and we made so many that we covered every wall of her room with them before she left, and when he came back my dad was like *whoa, that's a lot, how many fingers do you have?*"

This fond memory sent Benny into a fit of giggles so intense he actually doubled over.

Daisy laughed too, and instantly felt a hundred times better about staying.

"The paintings are not on the walls anymore," Dr. Webb

said, shaking his head as he watched his son's shoulders shake with laughter.

"You could cover the floor with them, and I wouldn't care," Daisy said. "I am plumb tuckered out."

"What does that mean?" Benny asked, popping up for air.

"It means I'm really, really tired," she told him.

"Oh. Well, there's definitely a bed in there," he told her solemnly. "I'll show you."

She glanced over at Dr. Webb.

He nodded.

When she looked back at Benny, he gave her an encouraging smile, grabbed her hand, and dragged her toward the back of the house.

"Plumb tuckered out," he said to himself, apparently trying it out.

Then he laughed again.

Will my little one be so lighthearted and sweet? she wondered happily as she let herself be led to the guest room.

2

KELLAN

Kellan watched after them, running a hand through his hair and feeling a little off balance. It was a lot to take in a stray when he was just getting his footing here himself.

But it looked like that was exactly what he was doing. No matter what the girl said about the inn, he could tell by her clothing that it was unlikely she could afford a long stay there. And with Frank's soft heart, Kellan figured he might have just landed himself a long-term roommate.

Your soft heart too, you idiot, he told himself.

It was true. The girl was disheveled, stressed out, and heavily pregnant, with a twang to her Pennsylvania accent that told him she was far from home.

Yet somehow, he had felt instantly drawn to her, almost protective...

You need to let your mom set you up, like she wants to, a little voice in the back of his head told him. *You just need a woman.*

He shook his head to clear it. That thought was obviously nonsense. What he felt for the girl was empathy, not attraction. And empathy was part of being a physician, a skill he had honed deliberately in order to improve his bedside manner.

Not that it had done him a lot of good. Getting the people of Trinity Falls to trust him with their medical needs when he had delivered their newspapers as a ten-year-old was turning out to be a lot harder than he expected.

Frank had originally hoped to retire and hand the whole practice over to Kellan as soon as he moved back. But now, Kellan was afraid the man would be stuck here forever, helping convince the seniors in town that the younger physician could still treat their diabetes and flu even though he wasn't silver-haired yet.

"Dad," Benny squeaked, "*Dad*, look at Daisy's pajamas."

He turned to find Daisy wearing a pair of white flannel pajamas with colorful dogs in Christmas hats on them. He had just picked up a pair in the same pattern for Benny last week.

"They're the *same as mine*," Benny said, his eyes dancing. "Can I go up and put mine on? Also, she has a *pie*. Can we eat pie?"

Sure enough, she was holding a pie in the distinctive Cassidy Farms box.

"I got it at the Co-op," she told him. "I thought maybe we could try it, if it's not too late for a snack?"

He was opening his mouth to say no when he noticed the hungry look in her eyes.

"Sure," he said, instead. "Go on up and change, Benny. Daisy and I will fix us each a plate."

"Okay," Benny said, dashing up the stairs so fast Kellan didn't have time to tell him to be careful.

"He's amazing," Daisy said, watching after him. "I can't remember, is seven-years-old second grade or third?"

"Second," Kellan said. "And if you bring it up, he'll tell

you *everything* about it. So, if you're tired, maybe save that conversation for the morning."

"Noted," she said with a smile, following him into the kitchen. "Is he always this enthusiastic?"

"He's an energetic kid," Kellan allowed. "But you knocked it out of the park with the pajamas and pie."

"I got lucky," she said with a smile. "And I'm sorry if it's impolite to be in my pajamas now. He was so excited when he saw me unpack them. I knew it would make him happy if I put them on."

He grabbed plates from the cupboard so she wouldn't see him smiling.

Not that she was going to get the wrong idea. She was expecting, after all. There had to be a Mr. Mullen out there somewhere.

He snuck a glance at her hands, but there was no ring.

Her hands are probably swollen from the pregnancy.

"Your other clothes were wet with snow. It's good you changed," Kellan said, grabbing forks and a knife and headed to the table. "If you want, I'll show you where the laundry is after we eat."

"That would be amazing," Daisy said. "By the way, your house is beautiful, Dr. Webb."

"It's Kellan," he told her.

"Kellan," she repeated carefully and softly, as if she wasn't really sure if it was okay to call him by his first name.

"And I can't take credit for the house," he told her. "Sadie Wilkinson decorated and furnished the place when she and Frank first moved in. Nothing's new, but it all wore well. I saw no reason to change it."

"She has timeless taste," Daisy agreed. "If it's not broken, don't fix it."

"My dad says that," Kellan said, nodding.

"So did mine," she told him. "He had about a million sayings. I wish I could remember them all."

"*Ta-da*," Benny sang out, running into the kitchen so fast that when he tried to stop in front of Daisy, he skidded like an ice skater along the polished wood floor. "Whoa."

"Careful, buddy," Daisy told him before Kellan could reprimand him. "There's only one of you in the whole wide world."

Kellan watched his son's smile melt from daredevil to lovelorn in less than a second.

"That's nice, Daisy," Benny said dreamily.

"Thank you," she told him. "Now I must say, you have excellent taste in pajamas."

He darted over to her, squeezing up to the side of her chair to push the fabric of their pajamas together.

"Incredible," she said. "If you sat in my lap you'd be perfectly camouflaged."

"I can't fit on your lap," he said. "You have a baby in your tummy."

"Benny—" Kellan began.

"Yes, I do," Daisy said in a pleased way. "And that makes me the luckiest lady in the world. Should I tell you when she kicks so you can feel it?"

Benny's eyes went big, and he nodded his head up and down.

"Don't worry," she told him. "It doesn't hurt a bit. Just feels funny. Like someone tapping your tummy from the inside."

"Wow," Benny said. "I hope she does it."

"Oh, she loves when I eat treats," Daisy laughed. "I'm sure she'll get right to work as soon as we get started on our midnight snack."

"Midnight snack?" Benny echoed.

"Well, it's not midnight," Daisy said. "But it's so dark outside, and it's way later than I normally eat. So, to me, it feels like a midnight snack."

Benny grinned at her.

"Here you go, son," Kellan said, placing Benny's plate at his usual place.

The boy scrambled up onto his chair at lightning speed, then looked dubiously at the pie on his plate.

"It's so small," he said sadly, resting his chin on his hands and peering down at it. "Why is my piece so small?"

"We don't want you having too much sugar this late at night," Kellan said. "You'll be bouncing off the walls."

But Benny had already lifted his head and was watching Daisy.

Kellan turned to see that their guest was eating ravenously. Half of the large slice of pie she had cut for herself was already gone, and her eyes were locked on the plate like she was afraid someone was going to try to take it from her.

She's hungry.

Instinctively, he moved to the refrigerator and grabbed the milk and a block of cheddar cheese.

He poured her a nearly-full mug of milk and slid it in front of her without saying anything.

Turning back to the counter, he grabbed a knife and cutting board and sliced half a dozen rectangles of cheese for her.

He brought them over and was pleased to see that half the milk was already gone.

But she was still knocking back pie like a bear coming out of hibernation. For such a tiny woman, she certainly had an appetite.

"I should have offered you dinner," he said, placing the plate of cheese beside her.

"Oh, wow," she said, looking up with an embarrassed expression. "I guess I just inhaled that pie."

He waited for her to take a piece of cheese, but she scraped her fork along the plate to pick up the last few crumbs instead.

"Mine's all gone too," Benny declared, wiping his mouth on his sleeve.

"Napkin, buddy," Kellan reminded him.

"Sorry, Daddy," Benny said, using his napkin to carefully clean off his already-clean mouth.

"Good job," Kellan told him.

"I think I need to get some sleep," Daisy said, letting out a massive yawn and stretching her arms up. "Oh, wait..."

One of her hands went to her belly and her face lit up.

"Benny," she whispered. "Come here, quick, put your hand right here."

Benny dashed over and put his hand very gently where hers had been.

His eyebrows shot up so fast it would have been comical, if it hadn't also given Kellan a lump in his throat for no reason he could understand.

"Isn't that amazing?" Daisy asked Benny quietly.

"Wow," he whispered back to her in awe.

"She's saying, *Howdy, Benny, nice to meet you,*" she told him.

"Hi, baby," he said earnestly to her stomach. "What's your name?"

"She doesn't have one yet," she said, shaking her head. "Maybe you can help me think of one in the morning."

He nodded his head up and down with an expression on his face like he was fully ready to take on this new and important responsibility.

"Why don't we carry our plates to the sink?" Daisy asked

him. "The sooner we do that, the sooner we can get on the train to Snooze Town."

Benny chuckled and made his dad proud by grabbing his plate and fork *and* hers.

"Oh, wow, thank you," she told him. "What a gentleman."

She finished her milk and hoisted herself out of the chair, carrying the empty mug and the full plate of cheese over to the sink.

"Just leave the cheese plate by the sink," Kellan told her. "I'll wrap it up for Benny's snack tomorrow."

"Thank you," she said, giving him a smile that made her look like a sleepy angel.

She gave him a little wave and padded back toward the guest room like she was asleep on her feet.

He trailed behind her, allowing his protective instinct a little leeway since she actually looked like she might pass out before she made it to her bed.

But before she made it into her room, Benny ran past him.

"Daisy," he called to her. "You didn't get a hug goodnight."

She turned with a smile and opened her arms to him.

Kellan watched with a fresh lump in his throat as his son wrapped his arms around the girl's big belly and hugged her close.

"Not too tight, buddy," he said after a moment.

"Oh, that was just right," Daisy said as Benny let go. "I'll sleep like a log."

"Like a log," Benny repeated, chuckling and she smiled down at him fondly.

"I'll help you think of a name for your baby in the morning," he told her earnestly. "Don't worry, we'll make sure she gets a good one."

He darted past his dad and a moment later, Kellan heard his footsteps on the stairs.

"Do you, uh, need anything?" he asked Daisy, clearing his throat.

The hallway suddenly felt too narrow, the sleepy mother-to-be a little too close.

"Just a good night's rest," she said softly. "Thank you again for letting me stay."

He nodded and turned away, resisting the strange urge he had to thank her back.

3

KELLAN

Kellan walked Benny to school under the ice-frosted branches of the maples that met overhead.

"What about Cinderella?" Benny asked suddenly, an excited look on his face.

"I think that's a good name for a princess," Kellan said. "But she may want to have a job one day."

"Tiana had a job," Benny said. "And that name works for a princess too, in case she wants to marry a prince."

"Tiana is a very pretty name," Kellan agreed.

Kellan tried not to let Benny have too much screen time, but he had been watching movies with his little cousins at his grandparents' house, and he had clearly been paying attention.

"Can you put Tiana on the list?" Benny asked hopefully.

"Sure, bud," Kellan said, pulling his notepad from his pocket and jotting down *Tiana* on a list of other names Benny had come up with.

It was pretty sweet how he had latched onto the idea of naming Daisy's baby.

They got to the front of the school, and Benny got a sad look on his face, like he always did when he had to leave his dad. Then he spotted a friend, and he was instantly buzzing with excitement.

Benny's mood swings and physicality sometimes reminded Kellan of a beloved golden retriever they'd had on the farm growing up. Artemis was always either splashing into the river and bounding between the banks, shaking herself gloriously and barking up a storm, or snoring on her blanket in the corner - with no apparent energy setting for anything in-between.

"Go on," he told the boy. "Work hard, and I'll see you this afternoon."

Just like the golden, Benny burst onto the playground, bounding toward his friends, and digging in his backpack for the latest magic trick he'd bought from the hobby shop with his allowance.

How the boy could believe in magic when his father had brought him up learning about science and medicine Kellan would never know. But it was a harmless enough hobby, and he would grow out of it in time.

Glancing at his watch, Kellan realized if he hurried, he would have time to stop in and check on Daisy before heading into the office.

His office was a glassy, modern addition on the back of the house, but Frank had cautioned him to always treat the office and house as entirely separate entities.

"Walk around the block before you come home, if you have to," Frank had said. "Just make sure home feels like home and work feels like work."

That was all fine and well until people knocked on the front door in the night when they really ought to have gone to the emergency room or the twenty-four-hour clinic out on Route One.

But Kellan didn't really mind. He knew money was tight for folks these days.

And besides, medicine was not just a job. It was his true calling. He'd known it from the first time he helped birth a calf.

His brothers had never wanted anything but to stay on the family farm, but Kellan had gone off to medical school after college, knowing he wanted to save lives.

Now that he had been in the field a few years, he knew saving lives didn't happen every day. But improving lives did, and it was just as important.

He thought about Daisy telling Frank about her LPN. A nursing degree meant that she must share his interest in caring for people. But how and when had she even finished the schooling for it? She looked so young.

Maybe she isn't as young as she looks.

He thought about the baby she carried, and hoped that was the case.

Then he remembered how frantically she had choked down that pie last night, and quickened his steps. He definitely wanted to get home in time to make sure she had a healthy meal in her before he headed to the office.

Arriving at his own front step, he hesitated, almost tempted to knock. He wouldn't want to frighten her.

Don't be ridiculous, he chided himself. *It's your house. Go in.*

He stepped inside and headed for the kitchen. If she wasn't up yet, maybe he could have a healthy breakfast waiting for her.

But when he arrived, he found her opening a box of convenience store cakes over the kitchen sink.

"Hey, don't eat those," he said gently. "I was just coming in to rustle us up some breakfast. How about eggs?"

She wrinkled her nose.

"Okay, I've got oatmeal, I think," he told her.

"I'm really okay with this," she said, indicating the box of frosted, cellophane-wrapped cakes.

"What about cereal?" he compromised.

"Fine," she said, setting her box down.

"Have a seat," he told her, feeling relieved. "I'll just fix us some tea."

She ambled over to the table and sat down, leaving her junk food behind, to his immense relief.

He filled the electric kettle and started getting their breakfast ready, glancing over now and again to his guest.

Unlike most of the young women he knew, Daisy wasn't fussing with a cell phone. Instead, she was reading the cover of his latest issue of *The Pennsylvania Journal of Medicine*, which was sitting on the table.

"You can take that, if you want," he offered. "I finished up with it yesterday."

"Really?" she asked, looking pleased. "They keep it in plastic at the drug store, so you can't read it without buying it."

Her cheeks flushed suddenly, as if she hadn't meant to blurt out something that made a show of how poor she was.

"The subscription is included in one of my professional memberships," he told her. "Seems unfair for nurses to have to pay for it when doctors don't. I'll save them for you after I'm finished from here on out."

He carried over a tray with the tea things, as well as two bowls, spoons, cereal, and milk.

"Thank you," she said, looking up at him gratefully. "For the magazines, and for breakfast."

"It's my pleasure," he replied, watching with alarm as she dumped two heaping spoonfuls of sugar into her tea.

Closing his mouth, he put a splash of milk in his own tea and poured out cereal for them both. It was bran flakes with dried fruit and nuts, more of a weekend cereal, but he figured all the sweetness of the fruit would appeal to her.

To his utter horror, she spooned sugar onto the cereal too, before adding so much milk you couldn't see the flakes.

At least it will dilute the sugar a little, his inner optimist pointed out. *As long as she doesn't drink the milk.*

She took a sip of her tea and moaned lightly in appreciation.

"It's chamomile," he told her. "No caffeine, so you don't have to worry."

"I think my dad used to make me this when I was sick," she said, taking another sip.

He nodded, feeling curious about her life back home. And what her bloodwork might look like, for that matter. And her teeth.

"What does your dad do?" he asked, figuring that was a light question to start off with.

"He worked in the mines," she said wistfully. "It was good paying work, but he started getting sick when I was in junior high."

"What kind of sick?" Kellan asked, his heart hurting for her.

"At first, we didn't know," she said. "Only that he got really worn out and couldn't catch his breath. He said he was just getting older, and so I started helping out with the yard work, and carrying in the groceries and all. But after a few more years, he couldn't work at all."

"Pneumoconiosis," Kellan said softly.

"Black Lung," she confirmed. "He always knew it was a

risk, but he used his safety equipment, and hoped for the best. He told me he didn't have a lot of choices, but he wanted me to get my education, so I would."

"Good man," Kellan said, his heart hurting for her.

"He was," she agreed.

"Is his death what brings you here?" Kellan asked. "You had mentioned him to Frank."

"In a way, I guess," she told him thoughtfully. "I'm sure you're wondering about the baby."

"I'll listen to whatever you want to share, but I'm not here to judge you," Kellan said. "You don't have to speak one more word."

"My boyfriend, Finn, was there for me when Daddy passed," she said softly. "He asked me to marry him as soon as my heart was beginning to mend. We had been together since we were kids, and it felt right to be part of a family again, instead of by myself. And, of course, by then I was realizing how much it took to run a household. We got married at the courthouse, and he gave up his apartment and moved into Daddy's little house with me."

Kellan nodded, glad she'd had someone to help her and share the burden of life.

"This little peanut was unplanned," she said, smiling fondly at her round belly. "But I know Finn would have been over the moon. He wanted a whole bunch of kids one day."

"Would have been?" Kellan echoed, dreading the answer.

"The mine took from me twice," she said simply, her voice strangely expressionless. "At least in Finn's case it was quick. One of the machines they use to carry coal out malfunctioned."

"I'm so sorry," Kellan breathed.

"You can see why I wanted to be as far from that town as I could get," she said softly. "I know it sounds reckless, coming all the way to Trinity Falls with a baby on the way, and no family here, but I just had to get that place behind me."

"That's not reckless at all," he told her. "You're trying to think of your baby's future."

"I thought of Dr. Wilkinson," she went on. "Daddy always spoke so highly of him, and I figured maybe he could use another nurse, or point me in the direction of someone else who could."

"Well, we decided to streamline the practice when Frank's regular nurse moved to be closer to her mom," Kellan said.

She nodded bravely, but he could see the dejection in her eyes.

"But we could use a receptionist," he heard himself say. "At least for a little while. Frank's regular receptionist retired, and no one seems to want to use the online portal we set up to replace her. Would you be interested?"

"Really?" she breathed.

The expression on her face was so filled with wonder that he found it hard to reply.

He nodded instead.

"*Yes*," she yelled, hopping out of her seat with one arm wrapped around her belly, and the other raised to the heavens, like she was a statue of a war hero or an avenging angel. "*Everything's coming up Daisy.*"

He couldn't help smiling back at her, his own heart pounding as if she had pulled him into her joyous orbit.

When was the last time I was that happy? he asked himself. *She has so much to mourn over, yet she allows her heart to be full.*

He tried not to let himself think about his part in that. He was doing no more than any decent person would.

"When you're ready, I'll show you the ropes," he told her gruffly. "Doesn't have to be today. You can settle in first."

"I do need to figure out housing," she said. "So, maybe I'll take today to do a little legwork on that."

"There's no need," he told her. "Of course, you can find a place of your own when you're ready, or when something you like comes up, but you're welcome to stay in the guest room free of charge for as long as you work for me. How's that?"

He knew housing in Trinity Falls was getting expensive. The rents were starting to drive out Frank's elderly patients in a way he wished he had the power to change.

But even if he couldn't change the whole market, he could offer a little relief to one young woman and the baby she carried.

"I know I should say no," she said, suddenly bursting into tears.

"You don't have to say no," he said, getting out of his seat and moving to her before suddenly wondering if he really ought to touch her. He was used to soothing Benny's heartaches with a hug.

She sobbed into her hands.

"The room is just sitting there, empty," he said helplessly, reaching out to give her an awkward pat on the shoulder. "Besides, Benny will get a kick out of having you around."

Before he could react, she was on her feet, wrapping her arms around him in a surprisingly strong hug.

"Thank you, thank you, thank you," she chanted into his chest.

He was momentarily lost in a haze of cinnamon scent and softness, then he pulled back gently.

"Has anyone ever told you that you wear your heart on your sleeve?" he asked her with a warm smile.

"I guess," she said, wiping her tears on the sleeve of her shirt.

"It's a good thing," he told her. "Don't ever let anyone tell you otherwise."

She gave him a teary-eyed smile that looked like the sun coming out from behind the clouds, and he felt something that had been stuck for a long time tear free in his chest.

4

DAISY

After breakfast, Daisy followed Kellan out through the side door on the kitchen and around the curved brick path to the glass doors on the office. The cold air cooled her cheeks, which were still warm from the little cry she'd just had.

It's okay to cry sometimes, she comforted herself inwardly. *Especially when you're happy. Besides, he's a doctor, and he's probably worked with plenty of hormonal moms-to-be.*

"Is there a door from inside the house too?" she asked, wondering what was the point of a convenient home office, if you couldn't get there from indoors.

"There is," he told her. "But Frank always recommended going outside on the way to and from work each day, so that's what I do. Unless it's pouring out."

"To make sure the entryway is nice and neat for patients?" she guessed.

"That's an excellent reason that I never thought of," Kellan told her. "But the reason Frank gave was that it's best to draw a line between your working life and your home life."

She nodded, and wondered if he realized that he had just demolished this important rule by inviting his receptionist to live in his house.

But he unlocked the glass door and swept it open for her pleasantly enough that she figured the significance of his kindness to her hadn't hit him yet.

If it does, I'll just go find an apartment. For now, I'm going to enjoy a well-heated house. All this warmth and good company has to be good for the baby.

She stepped into the office and had to smile.

The floor to ceiling windows all around made the place feel like a sunroom, overlooking the tree-lined backyard. Yet it was toasty warm inside.

"The glass is insulated with double panes," Kellan said. "And the heat is in the floor, so it rises. It was important to Frank that sick patients have a pleasant and comfortable space to wait in."

"It's really lovely," she told him honestly.

"Here's your desk," he told her, leading her to the back wall

There was a counter with a desk, and plenty of cabinets.

"I should probably start by learning the filing system," she said, indicating the drawers.

"Those are empty now," Kellan said proudly. "We're transitioning to a paperless office, so at least at the front desk there will be no need for filing anything physically."

"Wow," she said. "Dr. Wilkinson is ahead of his time."

"Well, that was my idea," Kellan said. "This is much more efficient and future-proof. Took the old receptionist forever to get everything scanned in, but it was worth it."

"I see," she said, trying to keep an open mind.

From her own experiences, she knew technology could be incredibly helpful and also incredibly finicky. Heaven forbid that the system decided to glitch and Kellan lost all his patients' important files.

"Now, why don't you have a seat?" Kellan offered. "I'll grab the stool from my office, and we can go over how the portal works."

TWO HOURS LATER, Daisy had three full pages of notes, as well as the book and troubleshooting guide that came with the software.

She generally did just fine with computers, but she could already see that the system wasn't especially intuitive. Which was probably why patients were having a hard time with it.

But she had to admit that it would be an extremely efficient system if all patients learned to use it. It was great for keeping track of medications, even including any possible interactions. And it logged all the notes directly into Kellan's files. If someone were seriously ill, it would be very easy for Kellan to send the entire file, including a log of all portal visits, straight to the hospital for them.

"Do you have any other questions?" Kellan asked her.

"Not for now," she said, shaking her head and looking down at her notes. "I'm sure I'll have more as soon as I start trying to use it. But for now, I think I've got it. Thank you so much for walking me through it."

"My pleasure," he told her. "I've got to head out on some house calls, but I'll be back in two or three hours. If there's a patient emergency, you can call or text, and I'll pick up."

"Will do," she told him, willing herself to stay calm and positive. Surely, there wouldn't be any emergencies on her first day.

"No one should be calling, since they've been told to use the portal," he told her slowly.

"But they might call anyway?" she guessed. "If they run into trouble with it?"

"Exactly," he said.

"Not to worry," she told him cheerfully. "I can walk them through the portal right on the phone. Once they have the hang of it, they'll be good to go for next time without help."

"I can already tell how helpful you're going to be," Kellan said warmly.

A burst of pleasure radiated through her chest, and she smiled up at him.

He gave her a little wave as he headed out the door.

And suddenly, she was alone in the big office.

She looked around, wondering what she was supposed to do when there were no calls. He probably didn't want to pay her to just sit around all day.

She wandered back to the broom closet and found a bottle of glass spray and a clean rag, and got to work cleaning the glass door.

It had been pretty clean already, but she decided it was better to keep busy than to get caught sleeping on the job.

When she was finished with the door, she got to work on the tables in the waiting room, and then the countertop and her own desk.

When every surface in the place was sparkling, and she was beginning to wonder if she should start on the windows, the phone rang. She picked it up right away, feeling relieved.

"Dr. Webb's office," she said. "This is Daisy. How can I help you?"

"Daisy?" the woman on the other end said, sounding confused.

"I'm brand new," Daisy confided. "And believe it or not, your phone call is my very first one. I really hope I can help you. That would be such a good omen for a new job."

The lady laughed.

"Well, my name is Margie Barrett," she said, sounding much more relaxed. "And I highly doubt you can help, but I hope you won't take it to heart."

"I'll try my best, Mrs. Barrett," Daisy said. "How's that?"

"It's perfect, and it's just Margie, dear," the lady said. "The reason I'm calling is that awful portal. My husband has bronchitis again, and I can't make heads or tails of the thing to set up a time for him to come in."

"I'm so sorry to hear that," Daisy told her. "Of course I'll help. Do you have the app for your phone?"

"Oh, no, dear," Margie said, in a way that made it sound like the suggestion was silly. "And that's a good thing, because if it was on the phone, I couldn't even call for help."

"Okay," Daisy said, hoping she was doing a good job keeping her smile out of her voice. "Are you at your computer now?"

"Sure am," Margie told her.

Daisy began walking her through the portal dashboard, but Margie stopped her right away.

"I'm in front of the computer," she said. "But I don't know where the portal is. Is it on my desktop or in my email?"

Daisy took a deep breath and proceeded to begin *really* at the beginning, helping Margie figure out which internet browser she had and open it.

After twenty minutes of intense work, they managed to get to the portal, realize Margie didn't know her username or password, and request a reset.

But the email address Kellan had on file for Margie was

an old one, and she had forgotten the password to it, so she couldn't retrieve the email reset for the portal.

"You know, they say the twenty-four-hour clinic out on Route One isn't too bad on price," Margie finally said. "And I can just call and set a time without all this hubbub."

Her tone was light, but her voice was a little shaky. And Daisy could hear Mr. Barrett coughing in the background of the call.

"I know Dr. Webb would want to help," Daisy said carefully. "He wouldn't want you to have to go to the clinic when you could set up an office visit or a house call with him."

Daisy paused a moment, torn between going against Kellan's wishes and losing one of his patients.

"We live two blocks away," Margie said suddenly. "What if I just brought my laptop over and you set it all up for me?"

"That would be using the portal," Daisy said carefully. "And that's what Dr. Webb wanted me to do. You know what? I think that's a great idea. Bring your cell phone, too. I'll try to get the app set up on there, so it'll be easier for you next time."

"Bless your sweetness," Margie said wholeheartedly. "I'll be there in five minutes."

Daisy hung up and hopped out of her chair, pacing around the office while she rubbed the stiff spot at the small of her back.

I'm helping patients use the portal. It's exactly what he wants...

But she wasn't a hundred-percent sure Kellan would be happy about it. He'd been pretty clear about how the patients were only supposed to communicate through the portal.

After a few minutes, the glass door swung open and a darling older lady with snow-white hair and a pretty blue dress with a purple shawl over it darted in, clutching an enormous laptop that was probably considered old for a computer while Daisy was still in high school.

"Oh, honey, I'm so glad you can help," she said, hanging the shawl on one of the hooks by the door.

"Margie?" Daisy asked.

"That's me," Margie said. "And you must be Daisy."

"Let's see what you've got," Daisy said, lowering herself to one of the sofas in the waiting room and patting the seat beside her.

Margie set her massive laptop on the coffee table and put her phone on top.

To her immense relief, the phone actually looked like a newer model, at least compared to the ancient laptop.

"That's a really nice phone," Daisy said.

"Oh, thank you," Margie replied. "My son gets a new one every year. Then he gives his old one to his wife, and she gives hers to my grandson. And then my grandson gives me his old one. So, you see it's practically brand new."

"That will work better than the laptop," Daisy told her. "If it's okay with you, I'll just get everything set up for you."

"Oh, wonderful," Margie said. "I'll just cheer you on."

Installing the app was no problem. Then Daisy got the new email address, typed it into the main computer to update it, and sent a new portal invitation.

"What was that?" Margie asked in alarm. "It's making a noise."

"That's the sound of an alert on the portal," Daisy told her. "It's inviting you to log in and set an appointment."

They both bent over the little device.

"Honey, my eyes aren't what they used to be," Margie said.

Sure enough, the font on the portal was tiny on the phone screen.

"Why don't I just handle it?" Daisy said. "I can ask you the questions and just enter the info for you really quickly."

They got started and almost immediately realized that the fields in the portal weren't actually large enough to input symptoms and notes.

"I can't tell it that he's coughing worse in the afternoons, huh?" Margie asked.

"Let's just say *cough worse in PM,*" Daisy said. "That it will take."

"But Dr. Wilkinson always asked what *kind* of cough," Margie said. "Like wet or dry? And how long had he been coughing for, and what had I done for him so far?"

"I know just what you mean," Daisy said. "Why don't you tell me all about it, I'll just take a few notes and then maybe I can slip them to Dr. Webb."

"Not if it gets you in trouble," Margie said. "He can just ask me in person."

"Okay, sounds good," Daisy told her.

They finished up their project, and when they were done, Margie reached over and gave her a hug.

"Thank you," she said softly.

"Come in anytime," Daisy said, hugging her back.

She watched the lady put her shawl back on and carry her giant laptop out the door again and then hoisted herself off the sofa and waddled back to her desk.

A moment later, the door opened again.

She looked up, expecting that maybe Margie had forgotten something.

But it was Kellan.

He was carrying a white paper bag. He shrugged off his coat and hung it by the door, then headed toward Daisy.

Had he seen Margie leaving?

Daisy held her breath and prayed that she wouldn't be fired on her first day.

"You did an excellent job today," he told her with a smile, setting the paper bag on the counter. "You know how I can tell?"

"How?" she asked.

"You got a call from Margie Barrett, didn't you?" he asked.

"Yes," she admitted.

"Well, I got an appointment request from her *on the portal*," he said with a victorious smile before she could confess. "I knew these old timers would come around once they realized how easy it was."

Daisy opened her mouth and closed it again, wondering what in the world she was supposed to do.

"I brought you a little treat to say thank you," he told her, patting the bag.

"Oh, wow, thank you," she told him. "You didn't have to do that."

But her belly was always feeling empty lately, so she grabbed the bag when he held it out.

"That's a really good salad," he told her. "The vegetables have tons of vitamins, and there's plenty of good fat and protein in it too - cheese and walnuts with grilled chicken."

She fought the urge to gag at the thought. Rabbit food with *walnuts*? Why couldn't he have brought her a nice cookie or something?

"Thank you so much," she told him, looking down at the bag in her hands. "You are such a thoughtful man, Kellan."

And it's the thought that counts, after all.

5

KELLAN

K ellan looked down at his new receptionist and couldn't help chuckling at the way her nose wrinkled when she looked at the food he'd brought her.

"The idea of that salad horrifies you, doesn't it?" he asked her.

She looked up at him, her expression ashamed until she saw that his smile was genuine.

"Sorry," she said with a sheepish smile. "Someone recently told me it was good that I wear my emotions on my sleeve, but right now I feel pretty spoiled and ungrateful."

"And I feel like a bad friend, pushing my food agenda on you," Kellan said. "Just remember, you're eating for two now. You have to make sure you're getting enough of the things you need for you and for the baby."

"Oh, we're fine," she said, waving her hand, like his suggestion was a fly she wanted to shoo away.

"When was your last prenatal check-up?" he asked her.

"I guess it's been a little while," she admitted, frowning.

"Why don't we do one now?" he asked as casually as he could. "I can just run some bloodwork—"

"You're worried, huh?" she asked, a knowing smile on her face.

She didn't look worried at all. As a matter of fact, it seemed a little bit like she was teasing him for being a worrywart.

But he found he didn't care. He wanted to check on her and the baby. If she was laughing at him, it was a small price to pay.

"Well, it's pretty quiet here today," he hedged. "We might as well get some use out of all this equipment."

"Fine," she said, hoisting herself out of the chair with a bit of an effort. "But I'm a little squeamish about blood."

"And you chose to become a nurse?" he asked.

"Just when it's mine," she clarified. "Other people's I can handle."

"I've got you," he told her. "You won't even have to look."

He led her back to his examining room, and gestured to the bed while he gathered everything they would need.

"How far along are you?" he asked her.

"Almost eight months now," she replied.

"And how are you feeling?" he asked.

"Pretty good," she told him. "No more throwing up in the mornings, thank goodness. I do get tired a little more easily lately. But overall, I feel great."

"That's wonderful," he told her. "Let's get your blood pressure."

They continued in friendly silence as he wrapped the sleeve around her arm and slipped his stethoscope inside before tightening it.

"Very good," he told her. "One-twelve over sixty-eight."

She nodded, looking pleased.

"Roll up your sleeve for me," he said lightly.

She complied bravely and without hesitation.

"At this point in the pregnancy, you're coming into the home stretch," he told her as he worked. "Of course, we always aim to get you both to the full term, but if she were born today, she'd likely be just fine.

Daisy's eyes widened at the thought.

"She probably weighs about five pounds, and she's just working on the finishing touches, like growing hair. She still spends most of her time sleeping, but she's also probably doing a lot of gymnastics in there."

"It's nice to think of her tumbling around," Daisy said, smiling up at him. "I used to love gymnastics when I was a girl."

It was hard to picture this very pregnant woman doing anything even remotely resembling gymnastics, but she certainly had the spirit for it.

"Okay, all set," Kellan said, removing the band from her arm. "You were a trooper."

"You're *done*?" she asked, her eyes widening. "I barely even felt it."

"Good," he told her with a smile. "Let's see how that glucose looks. We'll have the rest of your screening results later today."

"Okay," she said, rolling her sleeve back down.

He blinked at the result, unable to believe it.

"This isn't the same as a full fasting glucose test, but wow," he said. "Did you have any lunch?"

"You won't approve of what it was, but yes," she told him. "About an hour and a half ago."

He resisted the impulse to roll his eyes.

"It's okay, right?" she asked him.

"It's excellent," he told her, shaking his head. "One-oh-one. But I still think you could stand to cut back on the sugar."

"I'll take it under advisement," she laughed. "But just so you know, I doubt I could choke down half as much food as I do without it."

He laughed and walked back over to her, taking a seat on his stool.

"So, do you have any family medical history we should be thinking about during your pregnancy?" he asked.

"Well, you know what happened to the baby's father and grandfather," she said. "But those things aren't hereditary, thank goodness. Finn's parents are healthy. And my mom passed when I was really little."

"I'm very sorry to hear that," Kellan said, meaning it.

"Thanks," she said. "I don't really remember her. But she's the reason I wanted to be a nurse."

"Was she a nurse?" Kellan asked.

"No," Daisy said. "She stayed home with me, and before that she worked at a mechanic's shop. But she died of pneumonia. She didn't want to go to the doctor's because it was so expensive. By the time my dad realized how bad it was, she had to go to the hospital. They did what they could, but it was too late."

"Oh, Daisy," Kellan said, his heart breaking a little.

He had patients like her mother, but luckily most of their families would call him if anything got serious, and he would go to them, for free, if necessary.

"My dad always said the nurses were so kind to him, and tried so tirelessly to help her," she said. "I grew up knowing I wanted to be just like them."

"Nurses are amazing people," he agreed, feeling a little

guilty now for having told her he had streamlined the practice to eliminate the nurse's position.

But she only smiled and nodded.

"So, your dad brought you up on his own?" he asked.

Of course, he was thinking of Benny.

Technically, he and Bree had shared custody. But she chose to take her time with Benny less and less frequently.

It had started with her suggesting that he really shouldn't have to travel mid-week. Then she was only taking him every other weekend, then one weekend a month.

Kellan could pretty much map out how serious her dating life had gotten, based on when she stopped making regular plans at all, and only called for random visits.

After how she had dismissed him, and then Benny, too, he couldn't even bring himself to be curious about who she was trying to settle down with.

But he was willing to bet it was someone who valued material things as much as she did. That was one area where they'd never seen eye to eye. And by the time he'd realized just how deep the divide was, it was too late to do much about it.

He'd always kept things civil, for Benny. But he was never going to be close with his ex the way his brother seemed to be with his. He didn't know how Brody managed it, and he wasn't really sure if he envied it or not.

"Yes, and he was always an amazing dad," Daisy was saying. "He did everything a mom would do for me, including taking me out for manicures one time on my birthday."

"Really?" Kellan asked.

"Sure did," she nodded, her eyes dancing with merriment. "The girls at the salon fussed over him like he was royalty. And he loved it. I think if we could have afforded it, he would have taken me every week after that."

Kellan couldn't help smiling.

"*Dad*," Benny's voice came from the office entry. "*Dad, guess what?*"

"That school bus seems to come earlier every day," Kellan said to Daisy, shaking his head. "We're good here, but we can run a check anytime you want. *Here I come, buddy*."

"Thank you so much," she told him.

They headed out to the waiting room together, where Benny stood, clutching a brown paper bag.

"It was Mara's birthday," Benny said, practically bouncing in place. "And she had cupcakes for the whole class, and there was an extra one, and she said I could bring home the extra one. So, I brought it home for *you*."

Kellan smiled and waited for Benny to bring him the bag.

Instead, the little scamp darted right up to Daisy and held the bag out to her, as if it held the holy grail.

"Wow, Benny, really?" she asked. "For me? Do you think your dad might want it?"

"My dad only likes healthy stuff," Benny said, before Kellan could refuse. "You're like me. You have a sweet tooth."

She glanced over at Kellan, her eyes dancing again, as if to say, *This kid is the best.*

"I *do* have a sweet tooth," she agreed with a big smile. "Is it okay for me to dig right in?"

Benny nodded enthusiastically.

She reached into the bag and scooped out a vanilla cupcake topped with a crown of slightly smushed pink frosting that was bigger than the cupcake underneath.

"Oh, wow," she breathed in appreciation.

She glanced up at Kellan and then back down at her

treasure, shoving half of it in her mouth in one big bite, like she thought he was going to try to take it from her.

"Wow," Benny squeaked, sounding very impressed.

Kellan found himself laughing again. As a matter of fact, it felt like he'd been laughing since the moment he gotten home today.

6

DAISY

The next day, Daisy sat at the center of the sofa in the office waiting room. A happy patient sat on each side of her, watching her finish installing the portal on each of their phones and then use it to request annual check-ups.

"Margie said you could do it," Betty Ann Eustace said, patting Daisy's knee approvingly. "And here we are."

"All done," Daisy said, handing the lady her phone.

"Dr. Webb is so lucky to have your help," Ginny Davies said warmly from the other side of her. "I hope he's paying you well."

"I'm the one who's lucky to have his help," Daisy said. "Not only did he hire me, he's allowing me to stay in the guest room until I can find my own place. I just wish I could think of a good way to thank him."

Ginny gave Betty Ann a look over Daisy's head that she couldn't quite read.

"You're doing more than you know just by brightening up this waiting room," Betty Ann told her kindly.

Brightening up the waiting room...

The phone began to ring, and the ladies bid her a hasty goodbye before slipping their coats on and heading out into the wintry afternoon.

Daisy pulled herself off the sofa and headed over to the desk to answer the phone.

"Dr. Webb's office," she said. "This is Daisy. How can I help you?"

"Hey, Daisy, it's Kellan," a familiar, deep voice said.

She felt herself blushing, though she wasn't sure why.

"Hi, Kellan," she said softly, hoping her blush didn't show in her voice.

"I'm calling because I have a terrible feeling that you're planning to sit at your desk and work through lunch," Kellan said. "But I want you to take a real lunch hour. Go for a walk, eat something, read a book, whatever you want."

"That's so thoughtful," she said, feeling surprised.

She actually had been afraid to leave yesterday. It didn't seem right to lock up the office and not take the calls.

"Our outgoing message says there's a break at noon," he told her. "So, no one will be surprised. Besides, they can use the portal even if you're not there. I just got portal requests for annual check-ups from two of Frank's long-time patients."

That would be Betty Ann and Ginny.

She got a guilty feeling thinking about how much help his patients actually needed using the system. But there was no point saying anything to Kellan right now. Maybe once they got the hang of it, they would be able to do it on their own. Surely, he wouldn't be unhappy with her for getting them off to a good start by onboarding them. Wasn't that kind of why he'd hired her?

"Go eat lunch," he told her with a smile in his voice. "Humor me, and at least consider a lunch with something green in it?"

"I'm not promising you that," she laughed. "But I'll definitely try to have some fruit."

"Good enough," he declared. "See you this afternoon."

She hung up and looked around the office, taking in the space and the minimal areas of wall among all those windows.

The big, sunny space was cheerful, and also the tiniest bit stark. But Daisy was beginning to come up with an idea that could really brighten it up.

After a quick search on her phone to find the perfect place to pick up what she needed, she headed out the door, putting on her coat and locking up the office behind her when she left.

This time, she sat in the truck examining her directions before heading out. Trinity Falls village seemed to thin out quickly, giving way to more spread-out geography, and she wanted to have an idea of where she was going before she left the little town behind.

Once she was satisfied, she started the engine and drove off into the cold, sunny day.

The little village was so pretty. She drove slowly, since there were so many people out walking.

Beautiful Christmas decorations hung everywhere. Back home, she saw the same old plastic decorations trotted out year after year, sun faded and beloved. Here, many of the houses had fresh greenery and ribbons adorning their porches, as if they could afford to buy new decor every single year.

As the directions had indicated, once she was through

the village and past the community college campus, she headed left on Route One, where shops quickly gave way to woods on either side, and then a patchwork quilt of farmland.

In Daisy's hometown, the housing in the rural areas was mostly wood frame homes, in varying states of maintenance. Farms were more and more rare nowadays in her neck of the woods, and the farmhouses back home certainly weren't pretty stone or brick colonials, like the ones she saw here.

Money makes the world go 'round, Mr. Gilroy used to say with a creepy smile as he stared openly at her body while she was at the bank to deposit Finn's meager paychecks each month. While he amused himself staring at her flat chest, Daisy ignored him. She was too busy wondering how she was going to stretch that check through another month when the bills seemed to go up again and again, but the pay never did.

And heaven forbid the truck broke down again, or one of them got sick.

Too many of the young kids who worked the mine got desperate enough to take a loan with the PayDay Express across from the grocery store. But Daisy's father had told her it was better to do without food for a spell, to do without basically anything, than to promise away future earnings at the PayDay man's terms. He said money you got that way was as good as cursed for what it ended up costing you in the end.

These days I know more about cursed money than he ever warned me about...

But she put that thought out of her head as fast as she could.

Somehow, she had never been forced to darken the

threshold of the PayDay Express back home, although it always felt like they were on the verge of desperation. Most people she knew were in the same boat.

But this place felt different. She wondered if there even was a payday lender here. Based on the pretty houses and lavish Christmas decorations, she doubted many folks would have need of it.

Hopefully, that means Kellan can afford to keep me as a receptionist, she told herself. *If he does, I should be okay, even when the baby comes. Especially if I can find a cheap place to live.*

Though with the way the houses were kept, she was beginning to worry that a cheap enough place to live might not exist in Trinity Falls.

Do your very best, every day, her dad used to say. *And leave the rest in God's hands.*

She knew it was good advice, so she willed her heart to lighten. She would figure it all out in time. For now, Kellan had given her the blessing of a safe place to stay, and if she did her best, the rest would fall into place somehow.

Besides, who could feel down when they were in such cheerful surroundings?

She thought of Kellan's sweet patients, and how much she loved helping them, and immediately felt more like herself again.

She drove on for a few more minutes, the road winding around more pretty farms, until at last, she saw a wooden sign with apples and horses painted on it along with the words *Cassidy Farm.*

She turned into the gravel drive and was immediately impressed at the size of the place. The site had described it as a family farm set up for visitors to enjoy. She had pictured a little ranch house and maybe a hayride stand. But it was clearly a big step above that.

The gravel driveway looped up into two large parking areas. One was under the shade of two dozen sycamores planted in twin lines, their bulbous bark giving them character, even though their branches were bare.

There were signs for Pick-Your-Own fruits, another for the hayride, and then a huge area filled with fresh-cut Christmas trees, as well as a sign indicating that customers could opt to take a carriage ride to the hill to cut down their own trees.

Pretty fairy lights were strung throughout the tree section, and more lights lined the path to a massive octagonal stone barn with bins of greenery, holly, and bright red apples outside.

Between the two stood the huge glass nursery Daisy had come to visit.

She parked and got carefully out of the truck, sucking in a delicious breath of the fresh, cold air.

She glanced around the various offerings longingly, wishing she could explore the whole place. But her whole lunch hour would barely be enough time to get what she needed and hightail it back to the office.

So, she marched off toward the nursery.

She pushed open the glass door and was greeted by the scent of pine and berries. It instantly reminded her of a scratch-and-sniff book about a family of Christmas Bears that her father used to read to her. The memory had her smiling as she stepped inside.

"Welcome," a woman said cheerfully. "Can I help you find something in particular?"

The lady was short and stout, with silver streaks in her chestnut bun, and a smile so warm and friendly that Daisy felt like she was being hugged. She wore a bright red apron with a tag that said *Alice*.

"Hello," Daisy replied. "I'm interested in some small trees or house plants that are super easy to take care of. Do you have anything like that?"

She was stunned to hear herself asking for help. Normally she did her best to avoid salespeople.

"Of course," the lady said. "I'm Alice Cassidy, and I'll be happy to help."

"Alice Cassidy, as in Cassidy Farm?" Daisy asked.

"The very one," Alice said. "I don't normally work in the nursery these days, but one of our employees' children had a school performance today, and there was no one else to cover, so of course I'm here. It's nice to come back to my roots once in a while, no pun intended."

Daisy laughed as she followed Alice Cassidy further into the nursery.

"Now, does your home have lots of light?" she asked. "Or mostly shade?"

"This would actually be for work," Daisy told her. "It's a doctor's office, but there's tons of light, because the whole office is practically one giant window."

"You don't work for Kellan Webb, do you?" Alice asked.

"I do," Daisy said. "How did you guess?"

"That was about the best description of Frank Wilkinson's office I've ever heard," Alice laughed. "It is like one giant window."

"It's really beautiful just the way it is," Daisy said. "But I wanted to do something nice for Dr. Webb, to thank him for giving me a job and a temporary place to stay. And I thought some pretty plants to brighten up the office might be a nice way to say thank you."

"Oh, that's a wonderful idea," Alice said, clasping her hands together. "I've always thought that bright office would be a wonderful space for plants. Now, did you have a certain budget in mind?"

"I don't know if you really have much that would fit my budget," Daisy said, naming the modest amount she felt she could spend responsibly.

"Oh, we've got plenty," Alice said. "I've been trying to convince my nursery manager to turn over some of the inventory, so we have lots of choices on special right now."

She began leading Daisy around the store, grabbing a pull-cart and a strapping young employee to help them load it up.

By the time they were finished, she had two fiddle-leaf fig trees, with big, dark green leaves, and a big gorgeous potted Norfolk Island pine, all of which Alice assured her would thrive in the bright, indirect light of the office.

When they got to the checkout counter, Alice grabbed a couple of strands of twinkle lights from the display.

"These will look beautiful on them," she told Daisy. "And they're plain white, so you can leave them up after the holidays."

Daisy looked down at the three beautiful trees on the pull-cart and the special pots Alice had thrown on as well as the twinkle lights and she knew her budget wasn't enough, even if every single item in her order was on special.

"I have a confession to make," Alice whispered, leaning in over the counter.

Daisy met her eyes, wondering what in the world this sweet woman could ever have done to need to use the word *confess* about it.

"My husband Joe and I own this place," she said. "Joe Cassidy is the best thing that ever happened to me, and I'm as thrilled and amazed today that he fell in love with me as I was the first day he came courting."

Daisy grinned. She loved this kind of story.

"My husband is kind and hard working," Alice said. "He has a wonderful sense of humor and a heart of gold. *But* he doesn't like to slow down, and he doesn't like to admit he's getting older."

Daisy nodded. Her dad had been the same way, even when he was sick.

"Dr. Wilkinson was working patiently on Joe for years to get knee replacements," Alice went on. "And Joe was as stubborn as a mule. Wouldn't even hear the poor man out. But somehow, young Dr. Webb convinced Joe on his very first visit that it was time to get the surgery done. When Joe is healed up, I'll have my husband back for dancing, and I'll be grateful to Kellan Webb for the rest of my life for that."

"Wow," Daisy breathed.

"So, since I own the place," Alice went on, "you understand how I can discount anything I want, as much as I want. And now that you know the whole story, I'll bet you can see why I *want* to help you help Kellan."

"That's so wonderful of you," Daisy said.

Something about this situation was making her brain whir, and puzzle pieces click together in her heart, but she wasn't sure exactly why.

She was in awe of the way the older woman felt about her husband. It was all so romantic. What she'd had with Finn had been more like the logical next step in a good friendship. She loved him, of course she had, but it was something completely different than what this woman and her lucky husband had. The way Alice talked seemed more like something out of a movie.

Did people really feel that way about each other in real life?

Alice laughed and started ringing everything up.

"I'll be sure to let him know this is from both of us," Daisy added.

"Oh, no, dear," Alice said firmly. "I have a feeling Kellan will enjoy this surprise much more coming from you than from me. Besides, it's Christmastime, the perfect season for anonymous gifts."

7

KELLAN

Kellan pulled up in front of the last house of the day, feeling tired but determined.

While Frank had made house calls on request, Kellan had other ideas about how to incorporate house calls into caring for his patients.

Kellan had been an exchange student in Central America for a year in high school. The father of the host family was a doctor, and Kellan was amazed to learn that he spent a good portion of his time riding a motorcycle up and down the mountains to visit with his patients and their families.

One morning, over empanadas and coffee, he had explained to Kellan that he visited with each of his patients at least once every single year, whether that was in the office or in their home. He explained that just because some people didn't have the means to travel to the town center, and others wouldn't take the initiative, he was not relieved of his moral obligation to care for them.

Kellan had been struck to his soul at the idea that the

man felt a commitment to care that went beyond what his patients even asked for.

And now, Kellan finally had the opportunity to introduce that same standard of care into his own small community. It was a blessing that he hoped would make life better for each of his patients.

And he had reminded himself of that blessing as he pulled up to each and every single house, because many of his patients viewed his uninvited visit as an intrusion.

This will be easier each year, he told himself as he got out of the car and headed toward the front door. *They'll get used to it.*

He knocked, and after a minute or two, a woman opened the door.

"Kellan Webb," the lady said with a friendly smile. "What brings you here?"

"I'm making house calls today," Kellan said.

"That's lovely, dear, but no one here is sick," Mrs. Fitz said, looking at him oddly. "Maybe you got the name wrong?"

"Today I'm calling on patients Dr. Wilkinson and I haven't seen for a year, or who we're thinking about for other reasons," Kellan told her. "Mr. Fitz is on my list to chat with this afternoon. Is he around?"

"Sure," she said. "Come on in."

"Thank you," he told her, stepping into the living room.

"Hal," she called out. "Leticia's boy is here to see you."

"Wants three dollars for the newspaper, eh?" Mr. Fitz yelled back with a deep chuckle.

Mrs. Fitz smiled indulgently at her husband's teasing, and glanced over at Kellan.

He kept a straight face and ignored the joke. He needed to distance himself from people's memory of him as a paperboy if he wanted them to take him seriously as a physician, that much was clear to him.

"Send him back," Mr. Fitz yelled.

Mrs. Fitz walked Kellan back to a small den, just big enough for a love seat, a chair, and a television.

"Good to see you, boy," Mr. Fitz said with a friendly smile. "Have a seat."

Kellan chose the chair opposite the loveseat where Mr. Fitz sat, and Mrs. Fitz sat down beside her husband.

"What brings you here?" Mr. Fitz asked. "You having trouble with that truck of yours?"

Mr. Fitz had retired from the mechanic shop in town a few years back. But he had always been generous with help and advice to neighbors in need.

"No, sir," Kellan told him. "I noticed you hadn't refilled your blood pressure medication, so I brought along some free samples to tide you over until you have time to get to the drugstore."

He had practiced that line in the mirror until he could say it lightly enough that it seemed convincing. No man wanted another implying that he needed charity. But he knew money was tight these days, and medications were expensive. Several of his patients had been visibly relieved to get samples from him today.

Unfortunately, in this case, it would be pretty easy to see past his tone. After all, Gabriel's Pharmacy was only a few blocks away from the Fitz place, and Mr. Fitz was retired, with ample time to stop by.

"Oh, I've got plenty of those pills," Mr. Fitz said. "Save your samples."

"Are you not taking them because of the side effects?" Kellan asked. "We could try a different kind."

"Nah," Mr. Fitz said. "Honestly, I just forget to take 'em."

"I see," Kellan said, nodding and trying to hide his horror that a man could forget the pills that would add years to his life. "You could put an alert on your phone."

"I don't think my phone has that," Mr. Fitz said with a dubious expression, scratching the back of his neck.

"Why don't I take a look at it?" Kellan offered. "I can just put an alarm in for seven-thirty every evening, so you don't forget to take your pill after dinner."

"I'll grab it," Mrs. Fitz said brightly, running to the shelf by the television where an older model phone was plugged in.

"I don't really like that thing spying on me," Mr. Fitz said suddenly, glaring suspiciously at the phone in his wife's hand. "Especially with something personal like what pills I take. And that time's no good anyway. *Wheel* comes on at seven thirty."

"Hm," Kellan said. "Why don't we put in an alert at seven twenty that just says *Wheel of Fortune*? That way you can remember to take your medicine beforehand, and you'll never miss your show."

Mr. Fitz's eyebrows shot up at that suggestion and he nodded slowly.

"That's a wonderful idea, Hal," his wife said. "I hate to miss *Wheel*."

"That's the truth," he agreed. "Once in a while, we get to talking and forget to put it on."

"Okay, perfect," Kellan said, taking the phone from Mrs. Fitz and entering the alert. "How does that look?"

"Look at that, Lainey," Mr. Fitz said to his wife in a pleased way.

"I'm so glad you stopped by, Kellan," Mrs. Fitz said. "This was so helpful. Can we offer you a cup of coffee or something to eat? I made spaghetti for lunch. It'll only take a moment to heat you up a plate."

"No, no, thank you," Kellan said. "I'd better get on home before my boy gets off the school bus.

"Isn't that something?" Mr. Fitz said, shaking his head. "Seems like just yesterday you were on that bus yourself. Years start moving faster the older I get, I guess."

"Take care, Mr. Fitz," Kellan told him, getting up. "And take your medicine. I want you to have a whole lot more years, whether they're moving fast or slow."

Mr. Fitz chuckled, and Mrs. Fitz walked him to the front door.

"Thank you for coming," she told him softly. "That was very kind of you."

"It's my job," Kellan told her. "Call me if you need me, okay, Mrs. Fitz?"

"Will do, love," she told him, patting him on the arm as he headed out. "Send your mother my love, and tell her she should be proud of you."

He gave a little wave over his shoulder.

Overall, the visit had been a victory. The only trouble was that no matter how much he tried to meet his patients where they were, he still left feeling like they saw him as a little boy instead of a doctor.

At least he was close to home. And thanks to Daisy, it was unlikely that he'd have any phone calls to return.

After a short drive, he pulled up at the house and indulged himself in just one moment to close his eyes and take a deep breath.

The day had been challenging, but the worst was over. There were only a few more steps between this moment and his favorite part of the day - curling up with Benny to read to him.

Sure, those few steps included preparing and cleaning up after dinner, as well as convincing the little guy to do his homework and take a bath.

But Kellan had it under control. He was going to end the day feeling like he had left his patients better than he found them, even the ones who hadn't asked for help.

Yes, he had a lot of responsibilities in his life, but he was lucky that he had the capacity to fulfill them all.

Exhaling slowly, he grabbed his medical bag and got out of the car.

Following the path around back to the office, he noticed that Daisy was standing in the center of the waiting room instead of sitting behind her desk.

She probably just needs to stretch her legs, he told himself. *It's hard to sit all day, and even more so in her condition.*

But when he came in the door, he saw immediately what she had been doing.

Two massive plants and what looked like a living Christmas tree were set at intervals along the outside walls of the office.

"What's all this?" he demanded, feeling exhausted. "Who brought these?"

"Aren't they pretty?" Daisy asked dreamily. "They're a present."

"No," he stormed. "They're not pretty. They're just one more thing I have to take care of. And they're so massive that if one of them dies, I'll have to hire someone to cart it out of here. What kind of idiot gives someone something *alive* without even asking if they want it first?"

"Me," Daisy said, softly.

That single word hit him like a sledgehammer, and he finally turned to look at her.

She had gone pale, and her lips were pressed together, like she was trying hard not to cry in front of him.

Regret washed over him in a sickening wave, and he struggled for purchase.

He'd had the patience and humility of a servant all day long, and then ruined it all by being cruel to the one person who was trying to show him the same kind of care and kindness he had been showing to others.

He was as bad as the most ungrateful of his patients.

Worse, because he had been on the other side of it all day and should have known better.

Opening his mouth and then closing it again, he searched for the right words to express how wrong he had been to speak to her that way.

"I'm very sorry," she said tightly, before he could formulate a worthy apology. "I'll get rid of them myself. You're absolutely right, it was thoughtless of me to do this without your permission. Please go enjoy your afternoon. I'll make sure they're gone before the workday starts tomorrow."

"*Dad,*" Benny yelled from the front door before he had time to respond. "*Dad, I'm home.*"

Kellan glanced over at Daisy, but she was already heading back to her desk.

"Daisy," he said.

But Benny was already thundering into the office, arms outspread for his hug.

"Mara had two fruits with her lunch today," Benny said, in his most deliriously happy tone. "And she gave one to *me.*"

Kellan hugged him back, soaking in his son's happiness.

There was an awful lot of talk about Mara these days, and the girl seemed to have already figured out that the way to his son's heart was his stomach.

"Daisy," Benny yelled, letting go of his dad.

"I'm right here," she called to him from the desk. "I was just organizing a few things at the desk. How was your day?"

Her voice sounded cheerful enough, but Kellan swore he could hear just a hint of heartbreak in it.

"It was great," Benny said. "But I have to do my homework now."

Kellan suppressed a groan. He hated the new-fangled way the homework had to be done. It made the whole process seem like a chore.

"Come on, Dad," Benny said, waiting in the threshold.

Kellan tried to catch Daisy's eye, but she was focused on the computer screen and didn't look up. It was clear that she didn't want to continue their conversation.

At a complete loss, he trailed his son back into the house, hoping he could figure out how to right his wrong with a little distance.

8

KELLAN

Kellan kept one eye on the stove while Benny applied himself industriously to his homework.

The need to explain how he came up with answers to simple word problems would have driven Kellan up a wall, but Benny was clearly used to it. He was a bright boy and motivated. School was an easy place for him to shine, at least so far.

Kellan was grateful for that. With his new job demanding so much of his time, it was hard to garner the energy to cook, clean, and help Benny with homework. And of course, they had to have fun sometimes, too.

When the timer went off, he hopped up and scooped macaroni and cheese and steamed veggies onto two plates. It wasn't the healthiest dinner, but Benny loved the cheesy pasta dish enough to clean his plate, so Kellan had to take the win.

"All done," Benny announced, like he had just won the Kentucky Derby.

"Great job," Kellan told him. "Want to see if Daisy wants to join us for dinner?"

Benny darted back toward the office.

Kellan found himself holding his breath. Maybe she would see the dinner invitation as a gesture of apology.

But Benny came back alone, dragging his feet.

"She said she's not hungry right now, but thank you," he told his dad. "I shouldn't have told her about the vegetables."

"Vegetables are delicious," Kellan shot back automatically.

"I know that, Dad," Benny said. "But Daisy likes sweets."

"Okay," Kellan relented. "Go wash your hands."

"Okay," Benny said. "But did you see all the trees in the office? Daisy said they were there when I got home, but I was too excited to notice."

"Yes, they were there," Kellan said, hiding his smile.

"They're so cool," Benny said. "It's just like *Where the Wilds Things Are.*"

Kellan smiled openly this time. Benny was right, the little trees indoors, seemingly melting into the bigger ones outside the glass, really did give a feeling similar to the children's book Benny had loved so much.

"Wash up," he said again, feeling crushing guilt all over again for his reaction when he first saw them.

They ate quietly and then headed upstairs to read, which was normally Kellan's favorite part of the day.

After a couple of chapters of *The Wild Robot*, Kellan was tucking Benny in. But before he could give him the usual hug and kiss on the forehead, Benny pulled back.

"You're sad," he said, his big eyes solemn.

Kellan sat back on the edge of the bed and nodded slowly.

"I am sad," he acknowledged. "I didn't do a good job saying thank you when Daisy gave me those little trees."

"Like the time when Great-Aunt Fran gave me mustard for my birthday?" Benny asked.

"Yes," Kellan said, nodding. "Exactly like that. No. Worse."

Great-Aunt Fran had known Benny was in a phase where he loved mustard on everything back when he was five. But when Benny opened what he thought was a toy and found a jar of fancy mustard, he burst out crying and ran out of the room. Kellan had wanted to run out of the room too, in shame over his son's behavior.

And now he felt even worse.

"It's important to be grateful for gifts, even if you don't like them," Benny said earnestly, repeating Kellan's own words from two years ago back to him. "Because any gift shows that the person cares about you."

"You are one-hundred-percent right," Kellan said. "I wish you had been there to remind me."

"Are you going to write her a thank you note now?" Benny asked sympathetically.

Benny had written Great-Aunt Fran a thank you note after the mustard incident. When Kellan told him he had hurt her feelings, he had cried even harder. Kellan told him she would feel better if she had a note, and he had made Benny think of two nice things to say in his note - one about the gift and one about his great-aunt.

Though he hadn't enjoyed the writing part, the little boy's guilt had been visibly assuaged when it was done.

"I think I'll go talk to her in real life right now," Kellan said. "I don't want her to have to wait while I write a note. Plus, I don't know her address."

Benny laughed at the attempted joke, which lightened Kellen's heart a little.

"You should talk to her," Benny told him, getting serious again. "That's brave."

"You give excellent advice, son," Kellan told his boy. "Did you know that?"

Benny beamed up at him.

Kellan leaned down and delivered the usual hug and kiss, then stood and headed out of the room, stopping to give a wave and smile from the doorway.

"Love you, Dad," Benny said.

"Love you too, Benny," Kellan told him. "All the way around the world and back."

Kellan headed downstairs, and marched all the way to Daisy's room, knocking before he had the nerve to change his mind.

But the door hadn't been all the way shut, and it swung open to reveal that the room was empty and the bed still made from this morning.

His first thought was that he'd offended her enough to make her leave, but her stuff was still in the room.

It was too late for her to still be working.

But there weren't many other places for her to be. So, Kellan headed back to the office to look for Daisy, without a real plan as to what he might do when he found her.

9

DAISY

Daisy sat in one of the office armchairs, looking at the potted trees, and telling herself that everything was going to be okay. Somehow.

To cheer herself up, she had decided to turn on the twinkle lights and see how the little trees looked with them, even if they were only here for one night, and only one person got to see them.

They were beautiful.

Though she had expected the trees to look pretty all lit up, she hadn't anticipated the way they would reflect in the glassy walls of the office. To Daisy, it looked like an ocean of stars, a whole universe of softly twinkling lights.

Everyone she loved and trusted was up in the stars now. She wished they could tell her what to do, how to make things right.

She felt terrible about surprising Kellan with the trees. She had barely met him. Giving him a personal gift that came with a responsibility was overstepping in a big way, and she should have known better.

Maybe it was just wishful thinking, but she had felt a

connection with Kellan and his little family from the moment she met Benny and saw Kellan's whole self come to life in the presence of his son.

It was probably just her own loneliness telling her that they saw her as anything but a stranger in need. She was not a friend yet. She hadn't earned that. And her actions today meant it would probably take even longer than she expected to earn Kellan's trust.

But she still felt it was worth trying. She knew instinctively that he was a good man, and that eventually he would forgive her.

The real weight on her soul was stuffed in her old backpack, in the closet of her new room.

Though she tried to forget it was there, its existence seemed to bleed into every facet of her life, refusing to let go of her aching soul.

She had sworn she wouldn't touch it, that she would burn it, or fling it into the ocean, anything to escape its curse.

But none of those things felt right.

She had followed her heart this far, and wound up with a job and a safe place to live. Surely, if she kept listening patiently, her heart would lead her to the right thing to do with the contents of that backpack, and she would be unburdened at last.

In fact, Alice Cassidy had inadvertently given her an incredible idea, but Daisy wasn't sure she had the nerve to act on it.

Especially after today.

Just thinking about Kellan's words this afternoon had her questioning her judgement all over again.

She heard footsteps approaching and tried to shake herself out of her own head. It was probably Benny wanting to see the trees again. And now he could see them with the lights on.

His wonder had been such a joy to see that it made the whole mess feel worthwhile. Until she remembered his father's reaction.

"It's beautiful," a familiar deep voice said reverently.

"Kellan?" she asked, turning.

"Daisy, I'm so sorry," he told her, striding into the room and kneeling at the foot of her chair. "You did something very kind and thoughtful, for my patients and for me. And I was a monster about it."

"No, you were right," she said, shaking her head. "Plants are a responsibility. They don't make a good gift."

"My reaction had nothing to do with your beautiful gift," he told her. "I had a hard day, and I came home and took it out on you. I'm very sorry, and I promise you that it will never happen again, Daisy. I hope you can forgive me."

"There's nothing to forgive," she told him firmly. "And I'm getting rid of them tomorrow."

"Please don't," he told her, looking around. "I love them. And look how magical the office looks at night."

She looked around and couldn't help enjoying how beautiful the trees were with the lights twinkling like a galaxy. It was easier to enjoy them wholeheartedly now that he wasn't angry anymore.

He apologized.

In Daisy's experience, most men didn't have the capacity to say they were sorry. Even Finn had struggled with it.

Only the most confident and thoughtful of men had the self-assurance to admit when they made a mistake. Men like her father.

When she turned back, Kellan was gazing at her.

In the twinkling lights, his eyes were more intensely

blue than ever. The brilliance of the light played on the sharp planes of his jaw, and danced in his dark hair.

His eyes went slightly hazy as she gazed back at him, and she suddenly realized he was the most handsome man she had ever seen.

She felt a pull in her chest, like nothing she had ever experienced before, and her eyes went to his lips without her meaning to let it happen.

10

KELLAN

Kellan gazed at Daisy, transfixed by the expression in her beautiful brown eyes.

A ripple of desire tore through him, and he was so stunned by it that his breath caught in his throat.

She's so young, and a widow.

But he still felt a physical ache at the effort it took not to take her in his arms and press his mouth to that ghost of a smile on her plump lips.

Kellan hadn't felt this way about a woman in a long time. The desire was as unexpected as it was unwanted.

He deliberately raised his eyes to meet hers, away from that tempting half-smile.

She gazed at him wide-eyed, as if she had read his thoughts, and was scandalized by them. Or... maybe as if she had read his thoughts and was scandalized by her own reaction to them.

The air between them seemed to sizzle.

The chime of a cell phone cut through the silence, breaking the spell.

Kellan pulled back and straightened up quickly, shaking

away the inappropriate thoughts buzzing around him like swatting away a swarm of mosquitos.

Daisy stood, with some effort, and slid her phone out of her pocket.

He saw the caller ID without meaning to.

Quail Creek, Pennsylvania.

He stepped back a bit, waiting for her to either shut off the phone or pick up.

She looked down at the screen and seemed to waver.

"Go ahead, take it," he told her.

"Yes," she said. "I think I'll just..."

Then she was darting out of the office and heading through the house to her room, as if she didn't want him to hear any part of that call.

That was odd. Daisy seemed like such an open hearted, honest person. He wouldn't have pegged her as someone who wouldn't at least pick up and say hello while calmly walking away.

You don't know her...

He wanted to ignore the suspicious voice in the back of his head. But in this case, it was right.

Daisy had just walked into his life, yet somehow it seemed like she had always been here, like she was already a good friend and someone he cared about.

Maybe more than just a friend...

But the reality was that he had known her only a few days, and that she had arrived here in the middle of the night with nothing but a bag of clothing and a backpack. For all he knew, she was in some kind of trouble.

It made sense that he felt a connection when he saw her natural way with Benny. His son's happiness was the most important thing in the world to Kellan.

But if he removed himself from that context for a

moment, and looked at the situation on paper, he knew he would advise a friend to tread carefully and stay alert. And he had a feeling there was more to her story than she was letting on.

He slowly let out a breath and closed his eyes, willing his emotions to level out.

He had gone from fantasizing about kissing her and making her his own to envisioning her being involved in something terrible, all in the span of about three minutes.

The truth probably lay somewhere in the middle, and letting himself get riled up about it wasn't going to help.

You need to let your mom set you up with someone, the voice in the back of his head told him for the second time since Daisy's arrival. *You're so lonely that you can't think straight.*

But he liked that idea even less than before.

He opened his eyes and breathed in the sight of the twinkly lights and the light scent of pine, allowing all that beauty to soothe him.

Whatever else was going on, Daisy had done something nice for him. He was going to enjoy it for the kindness it was.

And he definitely wasn't going to wonder where she got the money for such a fancy gift.

11

DAISY

Daisy made it to her room and closed the door behind her before swiping to take the call.

Part of her was wishing he would have hung up by now, but of course he hadn't.

"Hey, Al," she said, bracing herself.

"Hey, Little Daisy Girl," her old landlord rasped, sounding pleased with himself for using his creepy nickname for her. "Where are you?"

"I cleaned," she told him. "The whole place is clean from top to bottom. And I left the keys on the counter for you, like I said in my message."

"I got your message," he said lightly. "You're not going to tell me where you're at?"

His tone was teasing, but she could tell he was serious. He really wanted to know where she was.

When her dad was around, Al had eyed her up plenty, but he never said or did anything inappropriate.

But as soon as her dad passed, he'd started coming around more often, giving her little presents to *cheer her up* and offering to work with her on the rent if she was having a hard time.

She never took him up on the rent offer. She might have been innocent in a lot of ways, but not so innocent that she could mistake what he was really trying to do.

And though she asked him repeatedly to stop bringing her gifts, he would get offended any time she tried to refuse one. *It's just candy*, he would say and march off with his nose in the air, making her worry he was going to jack up the rent or evict her if she made him angry. After all, it was her father's name on the lease, not hers.

Of course, she hadn't agreed to marry Finn just to protect herself from Al's advances, but if she was honest with herself, it had definitely been a selling point. But if she thought being married, or even pregnant, would slow Al down, she was very, very wrong.

When Finn passed, Al's advances had grown more aggressive.

And when word got out about what the mining company had done, she knew she had to get out before he came again.

So, she had loaded up the truck and cleaned the empty house as quickly as she could, without even waiting to hear back from the inn, or talk with Dr. Wilkinson.

If not for Kellan's kindness, running from Al might have put her in a worse position than she'd been in back home.

"I just needed some time away from Quail Creek," she told him. "After so much loss, it didn't feel right to stay."

"So much loss, or so much gain?" he asked, his voice cold now, and dangerous, like a snake waiting for a mouse to get too close.

That was too much. Fury rose in her chest.

"Why are you calling?" she asked, emboldened by the

distance. "The rent is paid up, and the house is empty and clean. I don't owe you anything."

"Is that so?" he asked. "Who cheered you up when your daddy passed? Who was good to you when your husband went and got himself killed?"

"I never asked for anything from you," she told him.

"You took it though, didn't you?" he said bitterly. "Now, where are you? I need a forwarding address, so I can mail the security deposit."

Daisy got a sick feeling inside.

Of course, he hadn't started off by telling her he needed to send her the security deposit. He'd backed her into a corner, forcing her to tell him she didn't want him to know where she was, and *then* revealing that she had to tell him anyway.

And now he was dangling the deposit. It was money that was rightfully hers, money that could help with everything the baby would need.

But there was no way she was going back for it, and it just didn't feel right to have it sent here. The last thing she wanted was to get Kellan mixed up in any of this.

"Keep it," she said, before she could change her mind. "Consider it payment for all those years of kindness. And consider our business officially done."

"Figures," he said with a dry chuckle. "Don't even need it no more, do you? Must be nice."

The hand holding the phone began to tremble.

"Goodbye, Al," she managed.

Daisy hung up and paced around her room for a few minutes, trying to shake the sick, hunted feeling.

It wasn't fair. She was hours away from the man. He shouldn't be able to make her feel like this—like the walls were closing in and she couldn't get a breath.

She went to the window and cracked it open an inch, letting the frosty air calm her a little.

It wasn't right to let the cold air into Kellan's lovely warm house, but she felt like her head might explode if she couldn't cool it a little.

Breathe, Daisy, she told herself. *Panicking isn't good for the baby.*

Everyone who knew her always thought she was the happiest, pluckiest person alive.

If only they could all see her right now, in a cold sweat, leaning against a cracked window as hot tears skated down her cheeks, scared of an old man halfway across the state.

I'm safe, she told herself. *I'm safe...*

But she couldn't seem to shake the feeling that no matter where she went, or what she tried to do with her life, deep down, she would never be anything but the kind of trash that guys like Al could push around and play with like a toy.

12

DAISY

Daisy woke before her alarm, wrapped in a blessed feeling of peace.

She opened her eyes to soft morning light pouring in the windows, giving the guest room an other-worldly feeling.

She had gone to bed last night trying to envision the future instead of getting bogged down by the past. It hadn't been easy to let go of her fears and hurts, but as soon as she was able to focus on the happier days she hoped were ahead, she found it easier to relax.

Visions of Kellan and Benny kept invading her fantasies of her happy future life, and she decided to let them. She told herself that she was picturing herself with Kellan's little family, enjoying morning walks in the park and afternoons baking cookies, because it was hard to picture the baby she hadn't met yet as anything more than a little bundle in her arms.

Before too long, she had drifted off into a deep and dreamless sleep.

And now she felt rested and calm, secure in her new life, in spite of last night's call.

She sat up, and her closet door creaked open.

It startled her a little, but nothing was out of place. She must not have closed it all the way when she went to bed last night. Her movement had caused the floorboards to shift slightly, that was all.

But the way the light was shining in the window, it almost looked like it was pointing *into* the closet. On the floor of the closet, in a puddle of brilliant sunlight, sat the backpack she had been trying to forget.

"A sign," she sighed happily.

In her heart, she knew it could as easily be a coincidence as a sign. But after a good night's rest and some perspective, she knew what she had to do.

If the contents of that backpack are weighing me down, then I have to empty it, she told herself fiercely. *No matter how long it takes.*

She approached the backpack gingerly, as if it might bite her, or set itself on fire.

Easing the zipper down, she opened the plastic grocery bag that was inside the backpack, and fished out one of the thirteen paper-wrapped packets.

With shaking hands, she opened it to find the stack of green bills with a paper loop reading $2,000 on it.

Those thirteen packets were what the coal company thought of as an even trade for the man who had been her best friend since she was a little girl—what they felt made up for their negligence—a payout of dirty, cursed cash for the widow left behind by their carelessness.

Even the company attorney had advised her quietly to seek her own counsel before accepting the proposed settlement.

But it had been all she could do to take their check. And she had strongly considered burning it or tearing it to shreds. Every instinct told her to keep their blood money away from herself and her unborn child. That money was cursed—she was sure of that much.

But a little voice in the back of her mind told her to cash the check, in spite of her fear and fury.

When they made a big announcement at the mines about the good they had done Finn's widow, she knew her time in Quail Creek had come to an end.

Al wouldn't be the only one sniffing around, now that folks knew she had that kind of money on hand.

The company had taken everyone she loved, and then effectively exiled her to keep her quiet.

But they couldn't take her integrity or her sense of self.

And her heart was singing with certainty today. She *could* spend this money without invoking its curse, so long as she didn't spend a single penny on herself. And so long as she was able to keep her gifts a secret.

She tucked the packet into her bag and said a silent prayer that she would be able to get rid of some of it by the end of the day.

THE MORNING WAS busy with Kellan seeing patients in the office. A few people stopped in to see her and ask for help with the portal. Apparently, word was getting out that she was the only one who could tame that particular beast. Thankfully, Kellan was in the back each time and only once caught her discussing the portal with a patient in person.

"I was just walking by," the man said defensively, when Kellan asked why he was there. "Was hoping to get a little help on that portal of yours, and I heard your Miss Mullen was a crackerjack on it."

"She certainly is," Kellan had said proudly before calling another patient back.

Daisy had sighed in relief before finishing up putting the man's appointment in. He didn't even have a phone new enough to download the app, so there was no way he could have done it himself.

When lunchtime rolled around, Kellan came out and reminded her to go enjoy herself for an hour. She thanked him, then slipped on her coat, grabbed her bag, and headed out into the cold, sunny day.

The air smelled like snow, and she smiled to herself as she walked down Columbia Avenue, heading past the Co-op grocery store toward the shops on Park.

Less than encouraging thoughts tried to invade her mind as she went, thoughts that told her that people here didn't have as many needs as those back home, or that she was kidding herself if she thought she could do anything surreptitiously, wearing her heart on her sleeve as she did.

But she didn't let those thoughts land on her. Instead, she kept her eyes open, waiting for a sign.

In the window of the real estate office, a woman was hanging a signboard with photographs of available houses. She was laughing as she tried to avoid the paper snowflakes hanging in the window.

Daisy decided to stop in and see if they handled rentals. She would need a place of her own before long. She waited until the lady had finished hanging the board and then pushed the door open.

There was a desk by the display window and another against the back wall, with a hand-knotted rug on the wood floor between them. Photographs of Trinity Falls over the years adorned the walls.

"Hi there," the pretty lady behind the front desk said. "I'm Sloane, how can I help you?"

"Well, hi there," Daisy replied. "I'm Daisy Mullen, Dr. Webb's new receptionist, and I'm interested in renting a little place, if you all do that sort of thing."

"We sure do," Sloane told her. "We don't have many rentals right now, but if you let me know what you're after, I'll write it down and be in touch when something pops up."

"That would be great," Daisy told her, trying not to feel discouraged. "My main concern is price, basically everything else is flexible."

Sloane asked her about her price range and her credit, then made a list for her of things that would help her when the time came, including gathering references.

Daisy tried not to think about what Al would say if someone called asking about her. While she had been respectful and always paid her rent on time, the man was a loose cannon.

I'll worry about it when the time comes, she told herself.

"Your price range will make this a difficult search," Sloane said carefully. "But I've never met a client I couldn't help out eventually. We will just have to be patient."

"I understand," Daisy told her, feeling grateful all over again that Kellan had offered her a place to stay until she could find her own.

"Now, if you're new to Trinity Falls, we can give you a packet of info about local activities, and even a Tarker County map," Sloane offered.

"Oh, I'll put one together right now," the receptionist at the back desk said with a smile.

When she hopped up, she caught her sleeve on her coffee mug, which crashed to the floor.

"Oh, no," the woman said sadly.

The pretty blue piece of pottery had cracked into a dozen pieces on the pine floor.

"Sorry, Anya," Sloane said sympathetically. "I know that was your favorite."

"At least it was empty," Anya said with a smile that didn't make it to her eyes. "That was a gift from a client my very first year here."

Daisy studied the fragments of the mug, memorizing the color. It looked handmade, and if she wasn't mistaken, the little art studio just down the street had similar pottery.

"Sorry about that," Sloane said. "Here's your list of things to do, and I'll just grab everything for a packet."

But Anya had abandoned her broken mug and was already heading over with a packet outstretched.

"If you need anything at all, just stop in," Anya told Daisy. "We're glad to help with housing needs, but if you want a recommendation for a dentist or a good place to buy party supplies or something, you can stop in for that, too. I'm the receptionist, so I'm here every day."

"Thank you so much," Daisy told them both.

"I'll be in touch when anything comes up that could work for you," Sloane told her kindly.

Daisy waved to them both and headed out into the winter afternoon again. Glancing at her watch, she saw that she had just enough time to do what she needed to do.

Lunchtime shoppers walked among the little storefronts, some of them pushing strollers and chatting.

That will be me one day. I'll be the one pushing a stroller and chatting with a friend.

Her hand went to her belly, and she felt a shiver of excitement to meet the little one.

The window of *Locally Made* was beautifully decorated with a mountain of cotton snow studded with pottery. The mugs and vases on display all held branches of holly and mistletoe. An old-fashioned bell dinged once as she pushed the door open and stepped inside.

"How may I help you?" the owner asked, looking over her reading glasses.

"I'm looking for a pretty mug for a friend," Daisy said.

She told herself it wasn't a real lie. She expected that she and Anya would be friends one day. After all, they were both receptionists in the same small town.

"How nice," the lady said with a big smile. "All our mugs are along that wall. They are all made by local artists. Let me know if you have any questions."

"Thank you," Daisy said, heading in the direction the lady had pointed.

The choices were endless. There were simple mugs, mugs with paintings and etchings, even mugs that seemed to have been formed with rolls of clay stacked on each other.

But in Daisy's eyes, one stood out from the others. It was just the right blue-purple swirl, like the one Anya had broken, and it had a good, sturdy handle.

Unlike the broken mug, this one had an etching on the side in the shape of a sweet little house.

"I like that one, too," the lady behind the counter said when Daisy picked it up to look at it.

"It's just right," Daisy decided, carrying it up.

While the lady carefully wrapped the mug in plain paper, and then in store wrapping paper, fussing over the handle and chatting about the artist, Daisy slipped a few bills out of the packet in her purse to pay.

"Here you are, dear," the lady told her a few minutes later, handing her the change, and the pretty package. "I hope your friend likes it."

"I'm sure she will," Daisy said. "Thank you for your help. I love your shop."

"I haven't seen you around before," the lady said, shaking her head. "You must be a student at the community college. We don't get near enough visits from you kids, I'm so glad you stopped in."

"I'm not a student, but I am brand new here," Daisy told her. "I work for Dr. Webb now, as his receptionist."

"Oh, are you the girl who is helping everyone get appointments?" the lady asked excitedly. "I want to get in for a check-up, but that portal thing is impossible."

Daisy glanced at her watch and decided she could make time to help.

"Do you have a cell phone?" she asked the lady. "If you want, I can set everything up and help you put in for your appointment."

"Oh, heavens, that would be wonderful," the lady said. "I'm Esther Jones."

"It's so nice to meet you, Mrs. Jones," Daisy said. "I'm Daisy Mullen."

Mrs. Jones slipped her phone out of her pocket and the two of them bent over it together. When the appointment was all set, Mrs. Jones gave Daisy the biggest smile.

"Isn't it funny, dear?" she asked. "He may be the doctor, but today *you* made a house call."

She laughed at her own little joke and Daisy laughed too, feeling more at home in Trinity Falls than ever.

When she left, the cold wind didn't feel so cold.

And the package with the mug in it felt just right in her bag. She hadn't gotten rid of much of that bad money, but she had ended up helping two people by doing it.

The only question was how to get the mug to Anya without her suspecting.

She crossed Park and headed back down Columbia as she tried to figure it out.

She could stop by after the office was closed, but plenty of people were always getting off the train and walking down Park. And most of the little restaurants were open for dinner.

No, she would get up early tomorrow and hang the bag on the door for Anya to find when she opened up.

A little shiver of anticipation went down her spine, and her heart felt light as a feather.

13

KELLAN

Kellan woke early, feeling the same happy anticipation he had grown accustomed to since Daisy arrived.

She had a way of setting him at his ease, and Benny, too. Though he was fighting tooth and nail against the attraction he felt for her, it was impossible not to be more relaxed when she was around.

Knowing how much she loved a good meal, he decided to make a big country breakfast, like his mom used to do on cold mornings.

He hummed to himself as he grabbed all the ingredients out of the cupboards, and had to chuckle when he realized he was humming *Joy to the World*. Kellan had never been big on Christmas carols. His brothers used to tease him for being tone deaf when he sang along in church.

Yet here he was, humming away, like the mysterious girl with the contagious smile had him forgetting all his foibles.

He had just gotten a tray of biscuits into the oven, and was flipping the crackling strips of bacon in the pan, when he heard the front door open.

He went still and listened. Though folks weren't overly security conscious in Trinity Falls, he always locked the doors before bed. Could he have been so distracted by Daisy that he had forgotten last night?

And who on earth would just *walk in*?

He was mentally running down everything within reach that could be used as a weapon when he heard soft footsteps and caught a delicate whiff of lilac shampoo.

"Daisy?" he asked.

"Hey," she said, popping her head into the kitchen.

"Were you out?" he asked.

She hesitated for a moment, with the strangest expression on her face.

For a moment, he almost wondered if she had been out doing something she shouldn't have.

"I was going for a walk," she said, without making eye contact.

"Good for you," he said, relief flooding his veins. He already felt silly for doubting her intentions. "It's wonderful that you're starting a healthy routine. You'll be more comfortable during your pregnancy if you give yourself lots of opportunities to stretch your legs."

She scowled at him.

"You don't like me telling you what to do, huh?" he chuckled, loving her straightforwardness. "Well, I'm a doctor, and sometimes I just can't help myself. But I'll try not to be so annoying. Ready for breakfast?"

"Breakfast," she moaned happily. "I changed my mind. You're not annoying at all."

"There's fresh juice in the fridge," he told her. "And if you want to grab the grapefruit that's in there, that would be great."

"I'll grab it," she said. "As soon as you promise me that's

real bacon in your pan, not some kind of bacon-shaped bean paste."

"It's real bacon, I promise," he laughed. "And there are homemade biscuits in the oven."

She smiled and muttered something to herself that sounded like *raised right* before opening the refrigerator to get out the rest of their breakfast.

He set the bacon on a plate and poured the grease into a can to cool. He was just cracking eggs into the pan when he heard Benny thundering down the stairs.

"Dad," Benny called to him before he had even reached the bottom of the steps. "I got up and brushed my teeth and got dressed already."

"That's great, bud," Kellan told him. "Because I made a big country breakfast."

"*Bacon*," Benny yelled, dashing into the kitchen.

"You're a boy after my own heart," Daisy laughed.

"Good morning, Daisy," Benny said, stopping to wrap his arms around her waist and give her a careful squeeze before he headed to his dad.

"Good morning, champ," she said, patting his head.

"Champ," he echoed in delight, grinning up at her.

"Is that a good nickname?" she asked. "I can try to think up another one, if you want. I just know you're the champion of magic tricks, so it seemed fitting."

Benny was so pleased by this remark that he seemed to actually inflate like a balloon.

"Can you set the table, Benny?" Kellan asked, before his son could float away.

They all worked quietly together getting the table set and the big meal laid out.

When they were all seated, he couldn't help noticing Daisy closing her eyes with a bowed head for a moment before she placed her napkin in her lap. Something about it tugged at his heart. Here was a young woman who took a moment to be grateful for all she had.

Benny regaled them with funny stories about school while they ate their breakfast, and Daisy laughed her head off at each one.

Between the fortifying meal and the lighthearted company, Kellan felt more ready to start his day than he had in a long time. He found himself wondering why he didn't cook a big breakfast every day.

But not everything was sunshine. He did have one thing to do this morning that he wasn't looking forward to.

"Benny," he said. "It's almost time to clean up and check your backpack, but first I wanted to ask you something."

"What is it, Dad?" Benny asked politely.

"I got a message from your mom last night," Kellan told him carefully. "She's interested in taking you to a hockey game as an early Christmas present. Would you like that?"

"Yes," Benny said, shooting out of his seat. "*Yes.* Did you tell her yes?"

"I will now," Kellan told him, hoping that Benny's happy anticipation would be rewarded this time. "But just remember that your mom's really busy. So maybe she can take you, and maybe she can't."

"This time she *can*," Benny decided excitedly. "And we're going to yell and laugh and eat snacks and have so much fun."

Kellan's heart ached, but there was no point taking away the boy's excitement. After all, with his mother's track record, the anticipation might be the only part of the gift he ended up getting.

"Okay, then," Kellan told him. "Let's get this table cleared."

As they worked together to carry in and wash up the breakfast dishes, he couldn't shake the sadness that had fallen over him.

Maybe this time she'll come through for him, he told himself. *He's so amazing. How could she not want to spend time with him?*

But, unlike Benny, Kellan didn't seem to have a pure enough heart to make himself believe in Bree over and over again without any encouraging evidence to back it up.

And he was beginning to think it was cruelty on his part to convey her messages to Benny. Maybe it would be better not to say his mother had been in touch at all until she actually showed up for him.

But that didn't feel right either.

One of these times, she'll see the light, he tried to tell himself. *It wouldn't be right to give up on her so much that I didn't even tell Benny when she messaged. She's his mother, after all.*

When breakfast was completely cleaned up, Daisy said goodbye and headed outside to enter the office from the glass doors.

Kellan smiled at the idea that she was taking Frank's advice, too.

He walked Benny to school, enjoying the boy's non-stop description of all the things he was going to do with his mother, which included showing her his latest magic tricks, telling her all about Daisy and the baby, and screaming for their team together while drinking root beer until he had a stomachache.

Kellan was glad that Benny felt comfortable talking to him about his mother. Kellan had tried hard to avoid the typical complaining-about-the-ex mentality and focused on helping Benny maintain as much relationship with Bree as she was interested in.

And he wasn't sure, but it seemed like Bree showed him the same respect. Benny never came home angry with Kellan or sullen.

Though he sometimes came home a little melancholy at the idea that he wouldn't see his mom for a while. She would talk a good game during their goodbyes, but it was usually at least a month or two before she made plans with Benny again.

On the way home from dropping Benny off, Kellan paused to text her back.

> I talked with Benny, and he would love to go to the game with you. Keep us posted on your plans. If you can't make it just let me know as soon as you can.

She texted back instantly, but that was her way when she took an interest.

BREE

> I'll be there. No ifs about it. Can't wait to see my little Benedict!

Kellan sighed and hoped it was the truth this time.

> By the way, he may mention that there's a woman living with us. She's my new receptionist and she's staying in the guest room while she looks for her own place. She's expecting a baby. I just didn't have the heart to make her stay at the inn.

> We're not together anymore. You don't have to explain anything. What's her name?

He growled at his phone and the two women passing him on the sidewalk exchanged a look.

> There isn't anything to explain. She's my receptionist. Her name is Daisy.

> Daisy Lee from Princeton Ave?

> Different Daisy. She's not from Trinity Falls.

> Where's she from?

> Quail Creek, I think.

> Oh, wow, nothing but bad news coming out of that place. She's lucky she got out.

> I've got to get to work, but let me know what time you'll swing by for Benny. He's really excited to see you.

> Will do!

He kept walking, wondering what in the world she meant about Quail Creek.

The town name had popped up on Daisy's phone last night, so he assumed it was a call from home. And the name of the place did sound familiar, but he hadn't thought too much about it.

On a whim, he decided to search it online and see if he could figure out what Bree was talking about.

He stopped on the corner before he got back to the

house, already feeling strange about searching Daisy's hometown like this, even though it was publicly available information.

I'm not stalking her, he told himself. *I'm just searching the town.*

He typed in the town name and a page of results loaded immediately. Most of them appeared to be news items.

And Bree was right, it was all awful:

Drinking Water Contaminated After Spill in Quail Creek, Pennsylvania

Faulty Equipment Suspected in Fatal Quail Creek Mine Accident

Embezzlement of Quail Creek Municipal Emergency Fund

He shook his head and sorted by most recent, which brought up another article:

$25,000 of Opioids Missing in Suspected Robbery at Quail Creek Clinic.

THAT MADE HIM SHIVER. Poor Daisy to have grown up in a place where so many terrible things were happening. And thefts like that most recent one would only get worse. With her being a nurse and working around medicines it was especially dangerous for her.

It's good that she got out, he told himself as he slipped his phone back in his pocket and headed for home.

Suddenly, Trinity Falls seemed more beautiful to him than ever. He drank in the sight of the sweet little houses on Columbia Avenue, the majestic bare branches of maples and sycamores meeting overhead, as if to shelter them from the rest of the world, with nothing but peaceful stretches of sleepy Pennsylvania farmland between here and Timber Run, where his parents sat in the sunroom now, sipping their coffee and talking quietly about holiday plans. His world was just as it had been every December for as long as he could remember.

It made his heart ache for Daisy, and for the other residents of Quail Creek, whose hometown was being wrested from them little by little with an unfair share of tragedy.

This is her home now, he told himself. *Trinity Falls belongs to those who choose it, whether they were born here or not.*

14

DAISY

Daisy had a productive morning at work, greeting and chatting with the patients who came in for their appointments. And she was even able to help a young mom download the portal and set up a house call for a houseful of sniffly children, all by phone.

Kellan came out just before her lunch break to remind her, as usual, that he expected her to take her whole hour and do something relaxing.

"Can I bring you back anything?" she offered, as she always did.

"No thank you," he told her. "Just enjoy yourself. Get to know your new town."

Though he was normally even more serious than usual at work, he gave her a gentle smile that seemed to make the baby in her belly do a summersault, but that was probably just a coincidence, or excitement for lunch.

My new town...

She headed out into the crisp afternoon sun with a little buzz of happiness in her heart.

The other night, she had sworn that something passed

between them. And then this morning, their breakfast with Benny had been so much fun.

It was hard to imagine moving out and looking for work as a nurse when pretending to be part of Kellan's family was so cozy. But she knew it was only temporary.

For today, she was planning to make another anonymous gift, if she could find the opportunity.

She walked down Park Avenue a bit, and peeked in the window of the real estate office.

A different agent was at the front desk today, but Anya was in her usual spot at the back, and Daisy felt a little shiver of happiness when she saw that the new mug was in a place of honor on her desk.

She kept walking, but there did not appear to be anyone in obvious need of anything on that side of the street, so she crossed and headed back toward Columbia Avenue.

The big windows of the Co-op gleamed in the sunlight, and she turned and headed up the steps to go in, knowing that Kellan would be happy to see her come back with a piece of fruit. Maybe she would even overhear a conversation that would lead to her next gift idea. The Co-op was always filled with chatting customers.

But before she even reached the bustling lunchtime interior of the store, she spotted a group of boys at two folding tables out on the patio, next to the Co-op's display of poinsettias. The boys had stacks of fresh pine wreaths, and there was a big donation can on one of the tables.

Daisy couldn't believe her luck at the opportunity to make *two* anonymous gifts at once.

She approached the table, and a little boy ran right up.

"Hello, ma'am," he said in a polite and cheerful tone. "Our local scout troop is selling wreaths to help a homeless shelter in the city. Would you like to purchase a wreath or make a donation? We can even deliver your wreath to anyplace in Trinity Falls."

"I would love to buy a wreath," she told him. "It's for a friend, but I don't want them to know it's from me. Is it possible to send one as a gift without saying who gave it?"

"Sure," the boy said, brightening up. "We put a gift tag, but it can say anything you want."

She followed the boy to the table and filled out the Wilkinsons' new address at the condos. She had been invited to stop by for tea, but since she was working, she hadn't made the time yet. Hopefully, they wouldn't guess that she was the one sending a wreath.

In the field for sender, she just wrote *Merry Christmas!*

She paid, and her hand was inches from the donation can, but she hesitated.

While she could put small change in that can without attracting notice, she wanted to do more.

But if the boy saw it, she felt certain he would get excited and that would cause the kind of attention she had to avoid when getting rid of the money.

He moved to attach her tag to a wreath.

"Wait," she told him. "Can you find one with a plaid bow instead of plain red? I think I saw one on that other table."

"Of course," he told her. "Wait here."

She made sure no one was looking before stuffing a thick wad of bills into the donation can.

A moment later, the boy was back with a wreath that had a red and green plaid ribbon.

"It's perfect," she told him. "Thank you so much for your help."

"Anytime," he told her, smiling so wide she thought it would hurt his cheeks.

She hurried into the Co-op, hoping to get in and out

before anyone noticed that donation can was stuffed practically full.

"Hello there, dear," a familiar voice said as soon as she stepped inside.

She turned to see Betty Ann Eustace, waving to her from one of the café tables where she sat with Ginny and another friend.

"Hello, ladies," Daisy said, hurrying over. "How are you today?"

"Very well, thank you, Daisy," Betty Ann said. "This is our friend, Shirley. Shirley, this is Daisy from Dr. Webb's office."

"I've heard such lovely things about you," Shirley said right away. "Would it be okay for me to stop in for some help with the portal?"

"Any time at all," Daisy said.

"Sit," Betty Ann said. "Have something to eat. We always get too much, and then we have to throw it away, which makes us sad."

"Oh, I shouldn't," Daisy said, eyeing the little table, which was practically groaning under the tray of sandwiches and cookies.

"You'll be saving me from trying to take them home," Shirley told her quietly. "I can't ever stand to see these pretty sandwiches thrown away, but they're always too soggy to eat for supper."

Ginny pulled out the empty chair next to her own and patted the seat.

The next thing she knew, Daisy was sitting down and being passed a plate with three sandwich halves on it and one massive, frosted cookie.

"Dr. Webb would cry if he saw me with this cookie," she confided, smiling down at the pale pink frosting in delight.

"He's too young to be so serious," Shirley laughed. "He needs to have a little fun now and then."

"Raising that polite little boy on his own is hard work," Betty Ann said firmly. "Better to be too serious, and teach the child his values."

"He's a wonderful father to Benny," Daisy said, looking through the sandwiches to find the one with the least green stuff on it. "The two of them are very happy, and Benny is such a nice boy."

She chose a grilled chicken breast with red peppers on sourdough and looked up to see all three women staring at her.

"What?" she asked. "I can't have food in my teeth already, I haven't even taken a bite yet."

"It's true, then," Ginny said, her eyes widening.

"What's true?" Daisy asked.

"You're living in the house with them, aren't you?" Betty Ann asked.

"Just until I can find a place of my own," Daisy said, feeling her cheeks heat with shame.

"When your husband gets to town?" Shirley guessed.

"My husband passed before he found out about this little one," Daisy said, patting her belly. "It will just be the two of us."

The ladies exchanged glances.

"You said Kellan is a good father?" Betty Ann asked.

"Absolutely," Daisy said, relieved to be off the topic of herself.

"We all consider him one of the most underrated bachelors in town," Ginny said with a twinkle in her eyes. "He's so handsome. Though I suppose he's a little old for you."

Of course he's not, a defiant voice in her head retorted.

"He's... he's my boss," Daisy said. "And I'm living in his house."

"That doesn't change whether or not you find him attractive," Betty Ann pointed out.

"You girls let her be," Shirley laughed. "Don't pay any attention to them, sweetheart. They won't be happy until the whole town is paired up like the animals on the ark."

"What's wrong with that?" Betty Ann asked. "Being paired up was the best thing that ever happened to me."

The women exchanged a warm smile with each other, and Daisy wasn't sure whether they were all amused at Betty Ann's romantic relationship with her husband, or if maybe he had passed, and she enjoyed honoring his memory by talking about him.

"Eat your lunch," Betty Ann said, turning her warm smile to Daisy. "I know he won't want you a single minute late back to your desk."

The women began discussing the upcoming Winter Wonderland Festival, and Daisy did as she was told and enjoyed her lunch.

The sandwich was delicious, and the cookie was absolutely divine.

It was only as she stood up to leave that she realized the table overlooked the patio out front.

Had the ladies seen her slip all that money into the donation can?

It was the perfect angle to see everything.

As Daisy headed back outside, she decided that she was pretty sure they hadn't. After all, wouldn't they have said something if they had?

15

KELLAN

Kellan stood in the kitchen, tossing the chicken wings he'd just taken out of the oven in a container of his mother's special sauce. The whole kitchen smelled incredible, just like he remembered from game days during his childhood.

Though he was an adult, and could make wings whenever he wanted, he hadn't thought to make the special meal on a regular night before. But in his quest to get a healthy meal into Daisy, he had remembered the irresistible chicken, and grabbed the ingredients after work.

Daisy herself was chopping celery, while Benny carefully poured blue cheese dressing into three little bowls.

"Not too much, buddy," Kellan reminded him.

"I know, Dad," Benny said. "About a quarter of a cup in each one."

"Whoa, you sound like a real cook," Daisy told Benny.

He grinned up at her, almost pouring the dressing onto the counter.

Kellan bit his tongue, wanting to see more of the two of them interacting.

If I have to clean blue cheese off the floor, it's worth it.

The thing of it was, Daisy and Benny seemed like they had been making dinner together every night of their lives. There was an air of lighthearted camaraderie between them that might have made Kellan feel jealous, if he wasn't so pleased to see it in the first place.

"Do we really need this much celery?" Daisy asked him suddenly.

"It's the only green thing on the plate," Benny told her before Kellan could answer. "So, yes."

He sounded so much like a small version of his father that Kellan burst out laughing.

Daisy and Benny both looked up at him in surprise.

"Sorry," he said. "It's just that I never realized I sounded like that, bud."

"That was a good laugh," Benny told him. "Your laugh is usually quiet."

"No it isn't," Kellan said automatically.

Daisy giggled and then Benny was giggling too, collapsing into her side in a cozy, snuggly way, without banging into her swollen tummy.

A little dressing dribbled on the counter, but Kellan couldn't bring himself to mind.

"I can't believe you two are laughing at me," he pretended to grumble. "Can't a man have a good belly laugh from time to time without being made fun of by his family?"

He realized too late that he had said *his family*, including Daisy in the mix.

Benny missed the context and just laughed harder.

But Daisy's eyes flashed to Kellan's right away.

He meant to mouth the word, *sorry*, he really did.

But there was a strange look in her eyes, a look that was almost... grateful?

So, he smiled at her instead, realizing that he was happy that she felt at home here, and that she would respond with that soft look when he said *family*. She needed all the support she could get.

"I think it's ready," Benny said. "But I spilled some."

"Don't worry, I've got you," Daisy told him, grabbing the sponge from the sink.

She tidied up the spill with Benny's help, while Kellan carried everything out to the table.

A few minutes later, they were all taking their first bite of Leticia Webb's famous wings.

"Mmmm," Daisy moaned. "So good."

Before Kellen had time to think about what that sound was doing to him, Benny let out a yelp, followed by a howl of sadness.

"Are you okay?" Daisy asked him.

"My tooth," he whimpered, his little hand cupping his mouth.

Kellan sighed. He had almost forgotten that the poor kid had a super loose tooth.

"Is it loose?" Daisy asked him.

"Really loose," he told her, tearfully. "We had corn on the cob at school, and I couldn't eat it. And now I have to miss Grandma's game day wings."

"Do you want me to get it out?" Kellan offered.

He already knew the answer. Benny really didn't like losing a tooth, and he would be too scared to let him take it out.

Benny shook his head hard, lips buttoned, like he was afraid his father would try to grab the tooth anyway.

"You know when I had a loose tooth, your uncles would tackle me and hold me down and Brody would just yank it out," Kellan told him.

"Sounds like a tall tale to me," Daisy said, quirking an eyebrow.

"I'm not going to visit Uncle Brody 'til it's *out*," Benny decided.

"I can just try very gently," Kellan offered. "And if it doesn't want to come out, it can stay where it is."

Benny shook his head.

"I guess you guys already tried the Tootsie Roll trick," Daisy said casually, looking down at her plate.

But Kellan knew she was bluffing because she was dipping a piece of celery in her dressing, and he knew how little interest she had in the celery.

"What's the Tootsie Roll trick?" Benny asked her, his eyes wide.

"Oh," she said, looking up. "It's almost like magic. You bite a Tootsie Roll and when you open your mouth the tooth is out."

Benny was leaning in, gazing up at her rapturously.

It reminded Kellan of the expression on his patients' faces as they stood around her desk, answering her questions and luxuriating in her friendly patter.

"I don't have a Tootsie Roll," Benny said sadly.

Kellan was almost taken aback. He hadn't expected the boy to be willing to try to get the tooth out, even with such a whimsical method.

"Oh, I have one in my backpack," Daisy said.

"I'll get it," Benny told her, hopping out of his seat.

"No, no," she said quickly, hoisting herself out of the chair in record time. "I'll get it. You sit here and repeat these words, *The Tootsie Roll trick works every time.*"

"*The Tootsie Roll trick works every time,*" Benny said, squeezing his eyes shut. "*The Tootsie Roll trick works every time.*"

A moment later, Daisy reappeared with a candy in her hand.

"Okay, which tooth is it?" she asked, as if she hadn't seen him wiggling it with his tongue for the last two days.

"This one, in front," he told her solemnly, pointing to it.

"Okay," she told him. "I'm going to unwrap this. You get ready to bite down."

He watched her like a hawk as she peeled off the paper and held out the candy.

"When I say *go*, you bite down hard," she told him.

"Okay," he told her excitedly.

"Three, two, one, *go*," she said.

Kellan watched as Benny bit down, barely missing Daisy's fingers.

"*I can't,*" he moaned, letting go of the candy. "It hurts."

"It's already out," Daisy told him, pulling it out of his mouth along with a string of drool and blood.

She ignored the sticky mess that had dripped onto her white sweater, and instead, held up the Tootsie Roll victoriously to him. "*See.*"

"*Dad,*" Benny yelled. "*It's out. Look.*"

He grabbed the candy, and was up and moving around the table, to show his dad the tooth, lodged in its chocolatey home.

"Get it out, get it out," Benny squeaked. "I want to *look* at it."

Kellan smiled and pried the tiny thing out of the candy. It was incredible that something so small could have been causing such a big fuss.

"Here you go," he told Benny.

Benny took the tooth *and* the candy, which he shoved into his mouth.

"You're going to eat it?" Daisy laughed. "You are one efficient kid."

"Did you want it?" he asked her, looking stricken. "It was yours."

"No, no," she told him. "When you do the Tootsie Roll trick you definitely get to keep the candy."

He smiled at her around his chewy treat with a lovelorn expression that made Kellan want to wrap them both up in his arms.

You're just responding to the fact that there's another adult in the house, he tried to tell himself. *It's good to have more than one person's perspective on how to help with tricky things like a loose tooth.*

But that wasn't it, not really. If he was honest with himself, he had to admit that he was responding to the fact that Daisy was there. Specifically Daisy, with her sweet smile her funny, straightforward reactions to things, and her heart, as big as the sun and just as warm, making his son feel like he was brave and capable.

She makes me feel that way, too.

"Are you ready to eat Grandma's famous game day wings now?" Daisy was asking Benny.

"*Yes,*" he replied.

She held up a wing, as if to toast him, and Benny picked his own wing up and smacked it to hers, sending a small spray of sauce onto her already messy sweater.

"I'm sorry, Daisy," Benny said, noticing her sweater.

"Oh, that's okay," she told him. "You can't eat good wings like these without getting a little messy. It's a compliment to the chef."

"A compliment to the chef," Benny repeated in delight, grinning at his dad.

"I'm the chef?" Kellan asked, which only made Benny chuckle. "Thank you, thank you."

He pretended to bow, and both of them laughed their heads off at him.

"Dad," Benny sang out rapturously.

Kellan got a happy, bubbly feeling in his chest. Had it really been so long since he let himself get silly?

Benny took a big bite of chicken, and Daisy smiled fondly at Kellan over the boy's head.

This is what I want, a quiet voice in the back of his head said. *I want this every night.*

16

KELLAN

W hen the meal was over, Kellan stood up and stretched.

He couldn't remember the last time he had lingered over dinner so long, chatting about his day with someone who was actually interested, while Benny leaned on his shoulder, listening contentedly.

Daisy appeared to be enjoying herself, too. Her sweet smile and easy laugh told him that she was relaxed.

"This was really nice," she told him, hopping up and grabbing her plate and Benny's. "Thank you."

"I'll clean up," he told her. "You go relax."

"No, no," she told him. "I think someone is ready for bed, and might need you."

She was looking at Benny, who did look pretty worn out. And if Bree actually showed up for him, tomorrow would be a big day.

"Ready for bed, bud?" Kellan asked him.

Benny nodded sleepily, and got up from the table to start his bedtime routine.

"I'll tell you when I'm ready for my story," Benny told

him, ending his statement with a big yawn before he headed up the stairs.

"Sounds good," Kellan said. "I'm just going to get these dishes done while you get ready."

Daisy was already taking a second trip into the kitchen, so he grabbed what was left and followed her.

They fell into their usual routine, with him washing and Daisy drying and putting away the dishes.

"I'm glad you're here," he heard himself tell her.

"Yeah?" she asked, her eyes twinkling.

"I grew up with so many siblings," he said thoughtfully. "I always wanted a little peace and quiet. But they were all really loud and zany."

"Not you," Daisy said without judgement.

"Not me," he agreed. "But I had to be even more serious in school. With all those rambunctious brothers, teachers wouldn't think I wanted to sit still and learn unless I really set myself apart."

"And you always wanted to be a doctor?" Daisy asked.

"Pretty much always," he told her, nodding. "Anyway, much as I like my peace and quiet, tonight made me realize how good it is to have a little company. It was nice to see Benny zone out and be the kid instead of having to hold up half the conversation."

Daisy laughed and went up on her toes to put a platter away.

"What?" he asked.

"I guess I never thought about it like that," she said. "I was the only one, with just my dad and me. And I loved talking with him. But I did always secretly wish for a big, noisy family."

Wait until I take you home for family dinner...

He was surprised at himself for that thought, though of

course there was no reason Daisy couldn't go to Timber Run for a Sunday night meal, after all, she was his receptionist, and his houseguest, and his friend, and maybe...

But that line of thinking would only twist his mind and heart.

"Was wishing for a big family part of why you decided to marry young?" he asked her encouragingly.

"I always had a picture in my mind," she said slowly. "I could just see a big holiday table with all the fixings, and people seated all around it—older folks, adults, little kids, maybe a dog sleeping by the fireplace."

"I know exactly what you mean," he said, stunned.

She was basically describing his own household meals growing up with all the kids, his parents, the grandparents, the dog, and whoever had been roped into stopping by to share in the meal that night.

"And as far as marrying young," she said. "I can't say it was because I was planning a whole bunch of kids or anything. Honestly, I don't think we could have afforded more than one or two on what Finn was making."

"So why did you?" Kellan asked.

"He was my best friend," she said, shrugging. "We knew each other forever, so he felt like home. I mean it wasn't like in the movies with a lot of romance and candlelight and butterflies in your stomach while you wait to see if he's going to kiss you or not. It always felt more like we were taking the next logical step, if that makes sense?"

Kellan nodded, listening, trying to understand.

"When I lost my dad, he proposed," she said. "A bunch of our friends had gotten married already. There's honestly not much else to do in Quail Creek."

Kellan chuckled.

"Finn was always good to me, and I miss him every day,"

she went on, shaking her head. "And I think I miss my best friend more than I miss my husband, if that makes sense. He knew me my whole life, and he understood me. It wasn't what I would call exciting, but it was good to have a partner. He always had my back."

Kellan nodded, feeling a lump in his throat.

"Was it the same with Benny's mom?" she asked quietly.

That assumption was so wrong that he wasn't sure how to begin answering.

"Sorry," she said. "I guess I shouldn't ask. You don't have to tell me anything about her."

"No, of course you can ask," Kellan told her. "But it was nothing like that with her. I was just realizing that I guess it was the opposite."

"The opposite?" Daisy asked, stopping in the middle of drying a pan.

"Well, it was all passion and fighting," he said, shaking his head. "She was only happy if there were big romantic gestures and fancy restaurants involved."

"Is that why it didn't work out?" Daisy asked quietly.

"I guess so," Kellan said. "She always knew my dream was to come back here and be a family doctor. But I think she figured once we got used to city life, I would want to settle there. Money and society matter a lot to her, and she wasn't exactly straightforward about that when we were dating."

"She just wanted to land herself a rich doctor," Daisy laughed.

"Well, she made a pretty big strategic error there," Kellan chuckled. "I worked in the city long enough to pay off the worst of my student loans. But when Frank called to say he was retiring, I knew I had to come back. It isn't about money for me. I mean, I need to make a living, but it's mostly about the people, healing them."

"I know," Daisy told him. "That's as plain as the nose on your face."

His chest felt like it was filling with helium. Somehow, that was the nicest compliment he had ever received.

"So, she didn't know you very well," Daisy went on. "Did she leave you because you were coming back here?"

"Yeah," he said, feeling ashamed. "I guess you had it right. It's better to have a friendship than a fiery romance."

"You deserve both," she said suddenly, gazing up at him. "You're a good man, Kellan Webb. You deserve it all."

Suddenly, he had a picture in his own head—a holiday table of their own, with Benny and all his cousins, Kellan's siblings and parents, and Daisy, with the baby in her arms and another on the way, his ring sparkling on her finger and a look of happy contentment on her beautiful face, knowing that she and the little one were ensconced in the safety and love of a big family.

He could see it as clear as day.

As plain as the nose on my face.

"Daisy," he whispered helplessly, getting lost in the warmth of her pretty brown eyes.

They were so close that he could smell the sweet touch of lilac, and practically feel her heartbeat.

Don't you dare kiss her. She relies on you for everything. It wouldn't be right...

He clenched his hands into fists to stop them from wrapping around her shoulders and pulling her close. He took a deep breath, giving her time to turn away.

Instead, her eyes widened slightly, and her pink lips parted.

Before he could take in what was happening, her hands

were on his chest and she was going up on her toes to press her sweet lips to his.

It was a soft, chaste kiss, but it sent lightning bolts of desire through him.

She was only exploring her feelings. She didn't realize she was playing with fire.

Need coiled in him with an ache that nearly made him groan.

"*Dad*," Benny yelled, his footsteps on the stairs above. "Do we have something I can put my tooth in?"

Daisy pulled back, a horrified expression on her face, as if she had only just realized what she was doing.

He could hardly blame her. He felt like he was under a spell himself.

But he didn't want her to feel bad about kissing him. He was so glad she had been brave enough to show him how she felt.

She turned away before he could meet her eyes, putting away silverware like her life depended on it.

"Dad," Benny said, running in before Kellan could speak to her. "My tooth."

"Here you go, son," Kellan said, grabbing a plastic sandwich bag from the drawer. "You can put it in this, under your pillow."

"The tooth fairy is coming, Daisy," Benny told her rapturously.

"That's great, Benny," she said warmly, turning to look Benny right in the eyes.

Benny wrapped his arms around her and gave her a big hug, then let go just as quickly.

"Come on, Dad," he said. "Let's go read. The sooner I go to sleep, the sooner I'll wake up."

"Okay, okay," Kellan chuckled, allowing himself to be led away.

He tried to look over his shoulder at Daisy on the way out of the room, but she was industriously putting away the last of the dishes.

When we're done with our story, I'll come and talk with her, he told himself. *It will give us both a chance to calm down and think.*

He got another flash of a future version of Daisy in his mind's eye.

She was wearing an alabaster gown and a happy smile.

17

DAISY

Daisy woke from happy dreams to find herself in the pretty guest bedroom of Kellan's house once more.

Every day she wondered when she would begin to take this comfortable home for granted. So far, it showed no signs of happening. She couldn't imagine ever not being grateful for a warm house and a full belly. Happy anticipation filled her chest every time she awoke in this soft bed. It was a great way to start a day.

Her good feelings dropped away like a stone when the memory of what she had done last night came back to her, and her breath caught in her throat.

Had she really risked everything she was thankful for in exchange for one impulsive kiss?

It was worth it, a little voice in her head sighed.

She was ashamed of her brash behavior. But that kiss... It had been just like in the movies. A shiver of rightness had gone down her spine from the moment her lips touched his. Her mind was filled with fireworks, and if someone told her that cartoon birds had flown around them carrying flowers and ribbons in their beaks while her eyes were closed, she probably would have believed them.

But was it worth risking everything? her wiser angels asked sternly.

The fact that she had practically run away to hide in her room as soon as Kellan was out of sight probably said a lot about how she really felt.

Not wanting to think about it, she hurried up to start her morning routine. As the baby grew, she found she was more uncomfortable in the mornings, the wee one was heavy against a full bladder, and her limbs were always stiff.

Her doctor back home had suggested that sleeping on her left side was best for the baby, so that was what she did, all night long, even when it was uncomfortable.

"You need room in there, peanut," she told the baby as she brushed her teeth. "I don't mind a sore hip."

Daisy had always been short and slender, but the doctor had promised that the baby would be just fine, so long as she ate and slept plenty and took her vitamins.

The hot shower felt incredible, and her tense muscles slowly relaxed. Showering was becoming a bit of a chore, but between the stretching to reach her far away parts, and the pounding of the hot water, she was feeling much better by the time she was through.

When she was dried off and dressed, Daisy faced herself in the mirror. She had no idea what kind of trouble that kiss had stirred up, but now she was going to have to face it.

Once, back when her dad was still alive, she had a rare fight with Finn. When she told her dad that she felt bad about the things she had said, he gave her a piece of advice.

Apologize, and then act like it never happened, he had told her. *Men don't like to dwell on unpleasantness, so don't turn it into a thing. Just apologize like you mean it, once, and move on without ever mentioning it again.*

It had worked then. No reason to think it wouldn't work again.

She nodded to herself and headed out of her room.

The house was blessedly quiet. She figured Kellan and Benny were sleeping a little late because it was the weekend.

Her own belly was rumbling. So, she headed into the kitchen, thinking of her heavenly TastyKakes.

But when she got there, she thought about how much Kellan wanted her eating real food for meals instead of treats.

A wonderful idea occurred to her. Why not cook a nice breakfast for everyone?

For a moment, she hesitated. Was it really okay for her to make herself at home in Kellan's kitchen? What if he was saving the ingredients she used, and he got mad?

Then I'll walk three blocks to the Co-op and replace them, she told herself.

She got to work starting a pot of coffee, that way if Kellan got up before she was done with the breakfast, he could have a mug.

Soon, the kitchen was fragrant with the scent of the delicious brew.

She grabbed ingredients for pancakes, deciding they would be easy to re-heat if the boys slept extra late.

The radio on the counter was too big a temptation to ignore. She turned it on very low, just for company.

"You're listening to WCCR," the announcer was saying. *"All Christmas music all the time, from November first to New Year's Day."*

Daisy smiled. She loved Christmas music.

"As you know, we're partnering with Robin Hood Jewelers on

Fifth and Walnut in Philadelphia," the announcer went on. *"With our help they're going to give away a one-carat diamond engagement ring this holiday season. So, keep listening to WCCR to find out how you and your special someone can celebrate this snowy season with some extra ice."*

She began mixing the batter, trying not to think about engagement rings.

Finn hadn't been able to afford one, and their wedding rings were the cheapest thing on offer at the local department store. But she had been proud to wear hers.

To Daisy, it wasn't about the jewelry, it was about knowing they had chosen to be loyal to each other.

Except you kissed someone else last night...

"I'm sorry, Finn," she whispered.

A sense of peace fell around her like a blanket, and she swore it was her best friend in the world, wrapping an arm around her, telling her, *Don't sweat it, D, he's a good guy.*

She knew it was only her mind, trying to help her survive the losses she had endured. But she wished Finn could really see her now, could know that their daughter would soon be born.

She didn't realize she was crying until a teardrop slid down her cheek and plopped into the batter.

Hurriedly she put the bowl down and grabbed a paper towel, swiping her eyes with it and begging herself to stop.

"Hey," a deep voice said from the doorway.

"K-Kellan," she said, looking up and feeling like the ugliest, most pathetic woman on the planet.

"Daisy—" he began, his voice full of sympathy.

"Wait," she told him. "Before you say anything at all, I want to apologize. My behavior was beyond inappropriate. You've been a model employer and a good friend to me, and I want more than anything for things to stay that way. I won't blame my hormones and emotions for what I did, because I'm an adult, and I should have some self-control. It was a momentary lapse in judgement that meant absolutely nothing. And I hope you'll accept my apology, because I mean it from the heart. I'm very, very sorry for what I did. And I hope we can agree to move on as friends, and never speak of it again."

He turned away from her, but not before she saw an expression of hurt, or maybe anger, darken his face. He crossed the kitchen and looked out the window into the trees that formed a border on the side of his lawn.

"That's really what you want?" he asked after a moment, still gazing out at the trees. "To forget it happened?"

No, but I'm not going to get what I actually want...

"More than anything," she said quickly, hoping he couldn't hear the note of desperation in her tone.

"Fine," he said, turning to her with a professional smile.

It was as if he had pulled a curtain across his face, and she had no clue what he was thinking or feeling. Was he still angry?

A frantic wail split the air and Kellan was moving faster than Daisy thought should be possible, taking the steps two at a time to get to his son.

She followed as quickly as she could, her heart pounding.

"Benny, what's wrong?" Kellan demanded as he flung the boy's bedroom door open.

"We've been robbed," Benny wailed. "There was a robber in the house."

Daisy's blood ran cold as she thought of the backpack in her closet.

If someone stole the money, I can never lift the curse...

"Why do you think that?" Kellan was asking calmly.

"Because I don't have my present," Benny said, tears flowing down his cheeks.

"What present?" Kellan asked.

"Last time the tooth fairy left me twenty dollars, and a really cool present," Benny wailed. "And this time there's only five dollars under my pillow. And no presents."

Relief flooded through Daisy, but she was still worried at how upset Benny seemed to be.

"We talked about that last time," Kellan told him, sighing. "We thought maybe that was a mistake on the tooth fairy's part, or maybe it was just a really special tooth for some reason. But twenty dollars and a card trick set is a lot more than the going rate. How would the tooth fairy even carry all that every night for all the kids who lost teeth?"

"Maybe if I sleep over with Mom tonight, the tooth fairy will leave my present there," Benny said, brightening and hopping out of bed. "Maybe she lives closer to the tooth fairy so it's easier to carry presents to her apartment. Maybe it will be a Switch this time!"

"You know that I don't want you having a video game system right now," Kellan said, his jaw tightening a little. "And the tooth fairy knows that, too. We were going to wait until you were a little older to talk about it."

"But if the tooth fairy brings it, then we don't have to talk about it at all," Benny said brightly, hopping out of bed and running off for the bathroom before Kellan could get another word in.

Kellan turned to Daisy with an embarrassed look on his face.

"His mother spoils him?" she guessed. "Since she feels bad for not being with him all the time."

"Something like that, yeah," he said, sighing. "Although when you put it that way, it doesn't seem so bad."

"There are much worse things," Daisy agreed.

"I would just hate for him to grow up being materialistic or entitled," Kellan said, finally meeting her eyes.

"I don't think you have to worry about that," Daisy told him. "He's a very sweet boy. As long as he has you to ground him and remind him of what's important, he'll be just fine."

"I brushed my teeth," Benny said, coming back in. "You still have to brush for the same time, even if you don't have as many teeth."

"Awesome," Daisy said. "Because I've got pancake batter ready downstairs. I hope you're hungry."

"Pancakes?' Benny asked with a big, under-construction smile, his tooth fairy robbery apparently forgotten.

"Yes," Daisy said. "And if you want, you can help me make them."

"*Yes*," Benny decided. "I'll be so fast getting dressed, you'll say *wow*."

"Okay," Daisy laughed. "See you down there."

She turned to see what Kellan thought of the nice home-made breakfast she was preparing, but he was busying himself with Benny's clothing and didn't even look up.

That's fine, she told herself. *It's great. It means he's trying to put things back to normal.*

But the sense of happy anticipation she had woken up with was gone.

It was going to be just a regular day, and there was nothing wrong with that. But then why did she have such a sinking feeling?

18

KELLAN

Kellan paced the living room, feeling like the walls were closing in.

Benny had taken a bath without being asked, and gotten dressed in his favorite jeans and sweater.

Now, he was sitting quietly on the sofa, looking at a storybook with Daisy. The two of them were trading off reading pages out loud and laughing at the funny parts, and the whole thing would have been the coziest scene in the world, if he didn't know what was really going on.

Bree was supposed to have picked Benny up over an hour ago.

And she hadn't been responding to Kellan's texts all day.

Meanwhile, Kellan had to administer flu shots in town tonight, and soon it would be too late to take Benny to his parents' place.

He turned at the front door and paced back toward the kitchen. But this time instead of turning again, he kept going, sliding his phone out of his pocket on the way.

Where are you?

BREE:

> I'm so sorry. Something came up. I won't be able to make it.

Kellan ran a hand through his hair and tried to resist the impulse to roar out loud.

> Look if you want, you can take him. Just print these out. And tell Benedict I'm sorry. I'll take him next time.

Three bubbles moved on the screen for a moment, then a PDF appeared with the title *Tickets*.

But of course, Kellan couldn't take him. He had to give flu shots tonight.

And going to the game wasn't really the point. It was Benny getting time with his mother.

> Do you want to tell Benny yourself? You can call.

> I'm out. Can't really talk.

Kellan slid the phone back into his pocket, ignoring the buzzing that continued.

He was proud that he had always treated Bree with respect and compassion. She was Benny's mother, and they were raising a child together.

But if he continued the conversation now, he wasn't sure he could hold himself in check.

"Benny," he said, heading back into the living room. "I have some bad news."

"*No*," Benny howled, the tears starting instantly.

"Your mom just texted me that she can't make it," Kellan

said as calmly as he could. "But that means you get special time with Grandma and Grandpa."

Benny adored his grandparents. Grandma made cookies every time he visited, and he loved helping Grandpa build things in the basement workshop. And a special visit without the other cousins would mean he was spoiled with their full attention.

But tonight, he had been planning to see his mom.

Kellan's heart threatened to break when Benny let his face drop into his hands and cried silently, his thin shoulders moving up and down the only evidence of his silent sobs.

"Can't you take him?" Daisy asked quietly, her hand moving to gently stroke Benny's back.

"I volunteered to give flu shots over at the condos during the board meeting tonight," he told her. "I was on the meeting announcement long before Bree offered to take Benny to the game. I can't really get out of it."

He didn't say it out loud, but this round of shots could save lives. All the folks who were willing to come to the office to get a shot had taken it back in the fall. So, the December crowd probably wouldn't be getting the flu shot at all if they didn't get it tonight. And this year's flu was a nasty one.

"I could take him, if you have the tickets," Daisy offered.

Benny stopped crying and peeked up from his hands.

"No, no," Kellan said. "It's a long drive, and the games are so crowded."

"I've never been to a hockey game," Daisy said, her eyes twinkling. "And I always wanted to. It's not a big deal to take a little drive. Besides, it's the weekend, and I've got nothing else to do."

"You've never been to a hockey game before?" Benny asked excitedly.

She shook her head.

"It's so cool," he crowed. "You get to yell and laugh and eat as many hot dogs as you want. You're going to love it."

Daisy glanced up at Kellan, her eyes like a puppy begging for a walk.

"You really want to do this," he realized out loud.

"Obviously," she said. "I mean, free tickets to a hockey game? With Benny? Of course I want to."

Then a furrow appeared in her brow.

"But, I get it that we don't know each other very well," she said quickly. "I understand if it feels like too much to let me take him to the city."

"We know you, Daisy," Benny told her encouragingly. "You're our roommate."

That made her laugh, and Benny laughed too, even though he obviously didn't really know why.

The sight of his son laughing with tears still glistening on his cheeks tugged at Kellan's heartstrings. It was true that he hardly knew Daisy, but everything he did know told him she was thoughtful and responsible.

"I'll print the tickets," he said gruffly.

"*Hooray,*" Benny yelled.

Daisy started cheering too, and Kellan had to hide his smile as he headed out to the office to print the tickets for them.

Having another adult around is good for Benny, he told himself.

He had been tortured all day by memories of Daisy's sweet kiss. It had been all he could do to sleep last night, and he'd been eager to talk with her this morning and explore their feelings together.

But when she said she wanted to forget it happened, he had to honor that.

After all, she was relying on him for housing and work right now. If he asked her to reconsider and she agreed, he would never know if it was because she was actually interested in him, or because she was afraid of being put out in the cold.

Add in her youth, her pregnancy, and all the loss she had experienced in the last two years, and he felt like the villain in a fairy tale for even going along with it when she had kissed him.

Tonight, seeing her with Benny, he was very glad he had held himself in check all day.

Being here was good for her, but he was beginning to think it was even better for Benny. The two of them had hit it off from the very first moment. And she had a silly streak a mile wide.

Kellan knew he was too serious, but it was hard to just *be silly*, even for Benny's sake. As much as he tried, it just didn't come naturally to him.

But he was finding it easier to join in when those two had already set the mood.

Entering the office, he headed to the computer, planning to print the tickets.

But he could see the shapes of the little trees in the darkness. Impulsively, he stopped and plugged in the cord.

The office was instantly illuminated in a magical glow.

He stood there hypnotized for a moment by the otherworldly beauty. Suddenly, he was a child again, gazing up at the Christmas tree in wonder. He was a teenager, standing under the stars at the lake on the very first night of the summer. He was right here, fulfilling his lifelong dream of being a family doctor in his own hometown.

This is what she brings to us, he realized, *wonder and joy.*

He hurried over to the computer and printed out the tickets on autopilot, while his mind was still lost in the realization that Daisy was special, almost like an angel had been sent to him and to Benny, to ease their hearts.

I won't mess it up, Kellan reminded himself firmly. *I won't ruin everything by falling in love with her.*

He just hoped it wasn't already too late for that.

19

DAISY

Daisy walked through the crowd with Benny's hand wrapped firmly in hers.

For the most part, people gave her a little space as soon as they saw she was expecting, which was really nice. The other really nice thing was the little boy beside her. Benny had been positively radiant with joy all night.

And he was right, they had yelled and cheered with the crowd. Daisy's voice was hoarse from so much screaming.

They were headed to grab some concessions now and she was looking forward to a nice cold Coke.

"What do you think about a drink and a hot dog?" she asked him.

He nodded his head up and down enthusiastically, so she shouted their order to the vendor as soon as it was their turn in line.

She had a cardboard container with their drinks and dogs in her left hand and Benny's hand in her right, and they were heading back toward their seats, when Benny suddenly tugged hard on her.

"Look," he said excitedly, pointing to a display of team jerseys. "Can we get one, please?"

"They're really cool," Daisy told him carefully. "And you asked in such a nice way. But these are really expensive."

"My mom always buys me a jersey," Benny protested, his voice nudging slightly higher in pitch, dangerously close to whining.

"That's really generous of her," Daisy told him. "And it's so nice that she has money for jerseys at the game. But I don't have money for jerseys. I did have snack money though, right?"

He clamped his mouth shut and nodded, looking like he was disappointed and ashamed of himself at the same time.

Daisy gave him an encouraging smile.

She remembered that Kellan had basically agreed with her guess about Bree buying stuff for Benny because she felt bad not to have him living with her.

That meant that Benny had been learning from her that spending money equaled love, or at least attention.

And that wasn't his fault.

"Come on," she told him. "Let's go chow down on our snacks."

"Chow down," he echoed happily, his bad feelings forgotten. "*Chow down*."

As they made their way back toward their seats, she slipped her hand in her pocket and grabbed the little wad of bills she had set aside when they came in.

Soon, they came to the kiosk with the banner announcing it was collecting donations for children in Pennsylvania's foster care system.

As quickly and surreptitiously as possible, she slipped the wad of bills into the donation box and kept walking.

No one called out to thank her, and she breathed a sigh of relief.

"Hey," Benny said. "Can I ask you something?"

"Of course," she told him, wrenching her mind from its celebration over her latest gift.

"You said you didn't have enough money for jerseys," he said. "But you just put a whole bunch of money in that box."

Panic shot through her, but she forced herself to take a deep breath.

"Let's just walk over here," she told him, pointing to a small alcove outside a door marked *Employees Only*.

When they were safely tucked away from the crowd, she bent down to his level with some effort.

"Money is a powerful thing," she told Benny. "It's not the most important thing, but without it, life can be really hard."

He nodded, his little forehead furrowed.

"When I told you I didn't have money with me *for jerseys*, that's exactly what I meant," Daisy went on. "Look at the banner on the booth where I gave that money."

"*Make the Holidays Bright for Foster Kids*," Benny read.

"Do you know what that means?" Daisy asked.

He shook his head.

"Foster kids don't get to live with their own families," Daisy told him. "Their parents can't take care of them for one reason or another, so the children go stay with another family, or in a facility. That's a big building with rooms that have beds in them, a little bit like a hospital."

Benny nodded, looking sad.

"Those kids have food to eat and a bed to sleep in," Daisy went on. "And that's *good*. But there's no money for anything extra. Imagine it's Christmas morning, and you think you won't have any presents."

Benny frowned, and she saw that now he had tears in his eyes.

"It makes me really sad, too," she told him. "Even when we couldn't afford presents, at least I had my dad to sing Christmas carols with, and go for a walk to look at the pretty lights. Knowing that those kids don't have special things *or* their parents really makes you wish you could do something to help, doesn't it?"

Benny nodded emphatically.

"Well, the people in this booth are doing something really wonderful," Daisy told him. "They're collecting money so the kids can have something special for the holidays - a toy, or special foods, or books and clothing. Can you imagine if you thought you wouldn't get anything special on Christmas, but instead you wake up and there are tons of presents under the tree?"

"That's why you gave them that money," Benny said, looking moved.

"That's exactly right," she told him.

"But why didn't you hand it to the lady, like everyone else is doing?" Benny asked, pointing at the kiosk. "She would have given you a little candy cane."

Sure enough, the lady was handing out tiny candy canes to people who dropped their change or a folded bill in the box.

"Because someone gave me this money," Daisy heard herself say. "And I have to do good things with it. But I don't want anyone to know it was me who helped."

"You don't want them to say thank you?" Benny asked, sounding confused.

"It's not supposed to be about me," she said. "It's supposed to be about helping. And there's something magical about helping without anyone knowing about it."

"There is?" Benny asked intently.

"There really is," she told him. "Do you want to try it?"

He nodded his head up and down excitedly.

"Okay, we're going to keep walking toward our seats," she told him. "When we're almost there, there's a man dressed up like Santa Claus ringing a bell. And he has a collection tin."

"Is he helping foster kids, too?" Benny guessed.

"He is collecting to help all kinds of people," Daisy told him. "The money in his tin will help provide hot meals for people who don't have a home, and it will also help pay for heating for people who have a home but can't afford to turn on the heat even when it's very cold outside."

Benny gave a little shiver in sympathy.

"If you want to help, you can put some money in that tin," Daisy told him. "And I can help by distracting Santa Claus, so he doesn't see you doing it."

His eyes lit up like they were about to pull a heist, and it was all she could do not to laugh.

"Okay, hold this very carefully in your hand," she told him. "You don't want to drop it."

She slipped him the wad of bills she had prepared in her other pocket.

"Whoa," he said.

"It's not ours," she reminded him. "We're just using it to do good in the world."

He nodded, an expression on his little face that told her he knew how important this job was.

"Okay, let's go," she told him.

They walked on, Benny was clutching her hand tightly with his free hand and the one with the money in it was balled in a fist at his side.

A few minutes later, they heard the ringing of the bell that signified they had almost made it to Santa.

"When I start talking to him, you make the magic happen," Daisy told Benny.

"Happy Holidays to you," Santa said in a booming voice.

"Thank you," Daisy said. "But I just have to ask you something."

"What is it?" Santa asked.

"Is your beard real?" she whispered loudly.

This Santa was on the young side, with an obviously *very* fake beard. His eyes widened and he studied her like she had lost her mind.

"Uh," he said.

She squeezed Benny's hand.

"Because, I know your eyebrows don't match your beard, but that exact thing happened with my grandpa," Daisy chattered quickly. "I mean, his beard isn't two feet long with curls or anything. But it's very gray, and his eyebrows are still a brownish color. What do you think?"

"What do I think of what?" Santa asked, looking more confused than ever.

But Benny had succeeded in slipping the money into the tin, and he gave Daisy a thumbs up, an expression of pure joy and wonder on his sweet little face.

"I forget," she said quickly. "Merry Christmas!"

She and Benny darted into the crowd before the confused Santa could question her further. By the time they got back to their seats, they were melting with delighted laughter.

"We did it," Benny kept saying, his tone telling her that he couldn't believe it.

"We did," she told him. "Now we get to imagine hungry, tired people coming into a warm cafeteria to enjoy a nice hot Christmas dinner together. And we can imagine people turning on the heat in their homes so they can sleep better."

Benny closed his eyes, and she saw the smile on his face as he pictured all of it.

This money is doing him good, too, she realized. *It's doing good for everyone who touches it. I wish you could see it, Finn.*

For the first time, thinking of what was in that backpack didn't make her feel cursed anymore.

It felt a lot like redemption.

20

KELLAN

K ellan loaded up three plates with scrambled eggs and fresh fruit, enjoying the conversation going on at the table, where Daisy was pouring juice for Benny.

"Remember when Kirkland scored that hat trick?" Benny asked her excitedly. "Grandpa says they call it a hat trick because scoring three goals is like magic. Like pulling something from a hat."

"*We've never seen Kirkland on fire like this before, ladies and gentlemen*," Daisy barked out in an announcer's voice.

"And, Dad, hey, Dad," Benny yelled. "I ate two whole hotdogs, *two*."

"Sorry about that," Daisy said. "He was super hungry, and I'm pretty sure I shouldn't actually be eating hotdogs."

"You ate candy instead?" Kellan guessed, quirking a brow so she would know he was only teasing.

"Busted," she said with a big smile on her face.

"Busted," Benny echoed in pure delight. "Busted, busted, *busted*."

Daisy smiled at him fondly and Kellan felt like his heart would break with the sweetness.

He carried their plates over, and felt a jolt of satisfaction when Daisy licked her lips.

"Looks amazing," she said, taking her seat.

"Fruit," Benny said happily.

Kellan almost felt guilty that he was more worried about getting fruits and vegetables into his receptionist than into his son.

But Benny had always been a healthy eater. Daisy definitely needed a little encouragement.

Today she showed a little more enthusiasm for her nutritious breakfast, stabbing bites of apple and orange and eating with gusto.

They were all enjoying their meal when Kellan's phone rang.

He grabbed it and walked over to the counter as he swiped to pick up.

"This is Dr. Webb," he said. "How can I help?"

"Oh, Dr. Webb, thank goodness," a woman's voice said on the other end. "This is Donna Greer. It's so early. I didn't think you'd be in the office yet. Thank you for picking up."

"It's not a problem," he replied, not bothering to tell her that the office number automatically forwarded to his cell phone whenever the office was closed. "What can I do for you?"

"It's Bud," she told him. "We're in West Virginia, visiting with the grandkids, and he forgot his blood pressure medication. I don't have a prescription, and I can't even remember what it's called..."

Her voice was despondent. Kellan knew she worried over her husband's blood pressure. Bud being without his meds was probably about the scariest thing in the world for her.

"That's not a problem at all, Donna," Kellan told her. "Hang on for one second, okay?"

"Of course," she said.

He pulled up the home screen on his phone, tapped the portal app, and entered Bud Greer's name.

"It's a small light-yellow pill that Bud takes, right?" Kellan asked. "Shaped like an oval?"

"Yes," she said. "My goodness, how did you remember?"

"It's in his file," Kellan laughed. "I only wish I had a memory good enough to know his meds and dose by heart. I'll email you a prescription, unless you want me to call it in for you or email it to a local pharmacy there, so they can have it waiting for you."

"Email is fine," Donna said. "My daughter has a printer. I can't tell you how grateful I am."

"Not a worry, Donna," he told her. "Enjoy your time with the kids. You two deserve it. The prescription will be in your email in the next two minutes."

He hung up and then tapped on the portal app again, going through the steps to update Bud's prescription, then emailed it to Donna.

When he looked up from his phone, Daisy was staring at him in awe.

"Did you just use the portal for all of that?" she asked, looking stunned.

"Sure," he said. "That's the whole point of it. I'm a family doctor. If I get a call from a hospital in the middle of Benny's soccer practice, I have to be able to transfer files and consult on the spot. Instant access to medical records could save a life one day."

Daisy nodded, a thoughtful expression on her face.

"It's also paperless," he added. "So, no one has to run around gathering up documents."

"Dad likes things to be modern," Benny said. "Right, Dad? It's hard at first, but it's worth it if he can take better care of people."

"That's it, son," Kellan told him, smiling at the idea that the boy had clearly been listening at all those family dinners they had shared with the Wilkinsons as he convinced Frank it was time to introduce a portal to their patients.

"Want to see a magic trick, Daisy?" Benny said, changing the subject on a dime.

"Sure," she told him. "I'd love to."

Daisy was game, as usual. She always wanted to see the magic trick, or go to the hockey game, or run into town for some fresh air.

While Kellan felt like he was constantly saying *no* to stave off extra responsibilities and nonsense, Daisy faced the world with a *yes* right on the tip of her tongue, locked and loaded and ready to fire.

"What?" she asked suddenly.

He realized he had been staring at her for too long, but he still couldn't seem to tear his eyes from her face, which was even more adorable than usual because of the inquisitive expression.

"I'm about to be late for work, aren't I?" she said to herself with a chagrined expression. "Benny, will you save that magic trick for me and show it to me twice the minute you get home from school? I am determined to figure it out."

Benny nodded and Daisy was out the door, heading back to the office before Kellan could even reply.

Both Webb boys watched after her for a moment in silence.

"I don't know how we got along without her," Benny said, causing Kellan to chuckle at the very grown-up phrase.

Me neither, son, Kellan thought to himself.

He wrapped his arm around Benny's shoulder and gave him a squeeze.

"I think she likes you a lot," he told the boy.

"It's nice for her to practice hanging out with a kid, since she has a baby on the way," Benny said thoughtfully. "I think she likes you a lot, too."

"Yeah?" Kellan asked, willing his heart not to pound too fast. "Why do you say that?"

"I don't know," Benny said, shrugging. "It's just that whenever you're around, she seems happy. And she has hearts in her eyes."

True or not, it was such a nice idea that Kellan felt warm inside.

"You're a really romantic guy," he told Benny. "Did you know that?"

"I guess," Benny said, shrugging. "I have to go to school now, right?"

Kellan watched after his wise seven-year-old as he carried his own plate to the sink and turned back to his father.

What if he's right?

But Kellan stopped that train of thought before it could leave the station.

Daisy had told him in no uncertain terms what she wanted. If he cared about her, it was his job to honor that.

21

DAISY

The morning melted away for Daisy as they welcomed a dozen younger patients into the office.

Kellan explained that at this time of year, the Trinity Falls young adults who went away for college or who were serving in the military usually came home. So, he had used the portal to find patients ages eighteen to twenty-three and contacted their families last month to invite them to come in for a complimentary check-up.

"Are you worried about them?" Daisy asked, trying to understand why he would dedicate so much of his time for free to people young enough to be healthier than most of the patients he saw day-to-day.

"Leaving home for the first time can be stressful," Kellan said thoughtfully. "Most of these young people are just fine. But once in a while, one isn't. And I think it's easier to talk to me than it is to talk to their parents, if they're feeling overwhelmed. There are good resources in Tarker County, but if they don't open up to someone to let them know they need help, the resources don't do any good."

"Wow," Daisy said.

"Besides, coming in when they're healthy gets them in the habit of having regular check-ups, even though they're not living at home anymore," Kellan said with a smile. "And that's a healthy habit that could extend their lives."

"You're a good man, Kellan Webb," Daisy said.

She suddenly remembered that she had said that once before.

Right before I kissed him.

Blood rushed to her cheeks, and she quickly looked back down at her computer screen, unable to focus on what she was seeing there.

"You're not so bad yourself, Daisy Mullen," he said quietly before heading back to his office.

Mercifully, another patient arrived to check in right then. And then another.

Half an hour before her usual lunch hour, Kellan waved goodbye to the last patient of the morning.

"Why don't you take your lunch early?" he suggested. "I've got a lunch meeting an hour from now. That way, one of us will be in the office until closing time."

Daisy smiled up at him. She was pretty sure any other boss would have told her to take half an hour and spend the rest of her lunch back at her desk. Even if it got her in trouble every time she said it out loud, she could still *think* to herself that he was a good man.

"Thank you," she told him.

A few minutes later, she was bundled up and stepping out into a beautiful winter day. Snow flurries drifted down, painting the grass white without sticking on the sidewalk yet.

She had already decided to grab lunch at the Co-op and

eat it at her desk, in case Kellan wanted to pop out earlier than planned.

The grocery store was bustling with shoppers, and she even saw some familiar faces who greeted her warmly.

"Hey Daisy," someone called out.

She turned to find Lucy, the girl she had met her very first night in town, waving at her. It felt like a thousand years ago, though it really hadn't been long at all. And it made so much more sense that she was Kellan's sister, and not Frank Wilkinson's. Daisy waved back and returned the friendly smile.

At the prepared foods case, Daisy surprised herself by grabbing a salad and a fresh whole wheat roll with butter. Maybe Kellan's healthy meals were changing her appetite.

But in the check-out line, she couldn't resist grabbing a box of tiny candy canes to share with Benny. They would remind him of the mission they had been on last night.

She smiled at the memory of his sweet face as he realized how special it was to make a difference with an anonymous gift. Which got her thinking about her next one.

There were no donation cans at the check-out, and no one on the patio steps.

On a whim, she decided to check out the town library. Maybe she would find inspiration there for the next gift.

And either way, she could grab something nice to read. The cold winter nights were perfect for curling up with a book, and she hadn't had time to pack any from her tiny book collection to take with her on her way out of town.

The library itself was a handsome brick building, with huge palladium windows overlooking Park Avenue.

She stepped inside and crossed the lobby to enter the library itself. The space was so different from the town library back home that she was almost afraid to go in.

Another patron approached from the other side, and Daisy had no choice but to open the glass door and let them pass.

"Thank you," the lady said to her as she headed out.

Daisy entered and looked around, taking in the vaulted ceiling and thousands of books.

To her right, there was a row of tables with computers. The wall that faced Park Avenue was made up of massive windows, overlooking the library's grassy lawn and trees, as well as the row of Tudor-style shops across the street. An empty space with a rocking chair in front of the window looked like the perfect spot for story time.

The stacks began to the right of the big windows, and went deep enough that Daisy couldn't even see the back wall.

And to her left, stairs led up to what looked like a children's section with rows of picture books, bean bags, toys, and two small desks with computers.

At the center of the library, a woman with long gray hair and purple-framed glasses sat at a big round desk, reading intently.

On the other side of the desk was a great big Christmas tree, hung with paper ornaments with names written on them.

Though she had meant to locate the romance section, and maybe a community bulletin board, Daisy found herself heading straight for the tree.

A small sign on the table beside the tree said:

Adopt a Family for Christmas!

Have you always wanted to play Santa Claus?
Now you can fulfill your wish and help a local family in need.
Just select an ornament from the tree and open it to find a
shopping list of just-right gift suggestions.
Ornaments show the number of family members, so that you can
select an ornament that fits your budget.
Feel free to adopt together with a friend or neighbor!
Wrapped gifts must be dropped off at the library with the
corresponding ornament by December 21st. A bin in the lobby is
available for after-hours drop off.

No time for shopping, but still want to help?
Donations will be used to provide food and gift cards to families.

THERE WAS a box for donations on the little table, which was conveniently located in the corner, where only people in the main section of the library could see it.

Looking around and seeing no one, Daisy slipped a wad of bills from her pocket and placed it in the box.

The usual sense of relief came immediately.

It was as if a weight of grief was being lifted from her each time she moved a little of that cash out of her possession and into a place where it could be a blessing to someone.

She looked at the tree again, intending to grab an ornament, when a happy thought occurred to her.

It would be so much fun to bring Benny back here and let him choose the ornament. Then they could shop together for everything the family wanted.

The idea of sharing that joyful activity with him made her smile.

Glancing at her watch, she saw that she still had time to find a book or two and make it back to her desk early, so she headed off into the stacks to see what was available.

22

DAISY

A little while later, Daisy was back at work and feeling pleased.

Kellan using the portal this morning at breakfast had opened her eyes to how incredibly helpful it could be. But there were still valid issues making it difficult for even tech-savvy patients to use.

In her spare time, she was putting together a polite message with some suggestions for the company that had developed the portal. With minor adjustments and an update, she felt the system would be user-friendly enough that many clients would begin using it.

It was a little wild to think about writing to the development company. But if she owned a business and a couple of small changes could make her product more effective and popular with customers, she would want to know about it.

Besides, she wouldn't send anything along without Kellan's permission.

"Howdy, there," an older man's voice boomed from the doorway. "We spoke on the phone."

"Hi, Mr. Willis," she said. "Come on in, let's get you set up in the portal."

"I don't know about that," Mr. Willis said dubiously. "I thought maybe you could just set me up an appointment yourself."

"I know it seems strange and difficult at first," she told him carefully. "But the portal is actually really wonderful. Once you join, Dr. Webb will have all your medical records accessible to him at all times, even if he's away. That way if you ever get sick or need something, he can help you right away, without you waiting for him to be back in the office."

"Oh," Mr. Willis said, his eyebrows going up.

"Just this morning, before he even got to work, Dr. Webb was able to use the portal to help someone get an emergency prescription refill in less than a minute," Daisy said, careful not to overstep by sharing any specifics about another patient. "Dr. Webb sure was thankful that patient was registered on the portal, so he could make sure they got their medicine right away. Heaven forbid, if the person hadn't been registered, and Dr. Webb was over at his mother's house or out of town for the day, the poor patient would have had to wait for hours."

"I'll tell you what, young lady," Mr. Willis said. "If you can get me registered, I'll do my best to use the danged thing."

"It would be my pleasure to get you set up," she told him. "And I can show you how to use it, too."

She got a funny feeling and turned around.

Kellan was standing in the threshold of the doorway to his examining room, smiling down at her.

She wasn't sure, but it really seemed like he had probably heard every word she'd said to Mr. Willis.

And clearly, he approved.

"Hi, Mr. Willis," he said. "You stopped in to get some help registering for the portal?"

"Sure did," Mr. Willis replied. "And your girl here won me over. She was telling me what you did for the fellow who needed a prescription this morning."

"Sometimes, it can feel like technology makes things less personal," Kellan said. "But in that situation, I was relieved to have everything the patient needed, right there in my phone."

Mr. Willis nodded thoughtfully.

"Is it okay for me to steal Daisy's attention for a moment?" Kellan asked.

"Of course," Mr. Willis told him.

"Daisy, my lunch meeting today may go long," Kellan said. "Do you think you could hold down the fort? I'll have my mom come by to pick Benny up after school."

"Not a problem," she told him. "And I was going to ask you if I could borrow Benny this afternoon. I'm going to go to the mall, and I thought he might like to come along and see all the holiday decorations."

"I couldn't ask you to do that," Kellan said immediately.

"You're not asking me," she laughed. "I'm asking you."

"Well, sure," he said. "That's really nice of you."

"My pleasure," she said with a smile.

"She's all yours," he told Mr. Willis. "Thanks for letting me cut in for a minute there."

Before Kellan could step away, the door opened, and a woman breezed in.

She was tall and slender, with a mane of honey-blonde hair. Her short black skirt showed off a pair of long legs encased in black tights. And the top button of her blue satin blouse was unbuttoned. Daisy didn't know much about fashion, but she guessed the woman's shoes and bag were probably worth more than she made in a month.

"Kellan," the woman said in a throaty, sexy voice. "It's so nice to see you. Ready for lunch?"

Jealousy pierced Daisy's chest like a flaming arrow, shocking her so much that she was barely able to stifle a gasp of agony.

"Yes, of course," Kellan said. "Let me grab my coat."

He headed to the hooks on the wall as Daisy stared after him.

"Hey there, I'm Aimee," the woman said to Daisy in her lovely voice.

"Daisy," she replied stupidly, noticing for the first time in her life how plain her voice was.

At least Aimee didn't try to walk over and shake hands. Daisy was already feeling shorter than usual and as big as a house.

"Daisy is the new receptionist I told you about," Kellan said to Aimee as he held the door open for her.

"I'm glad you have a receptionist again," Aimee teased. "I thought you were trying to go off the grid or something."

She laughed a husky laugh and Kellan joined her.

A moment later, they were gone.

"You okay?" Mr. Willis asked sympathetically. "You look like the cheese fell off your cracker."

"Oh, I'm fine," she said, feeling her cheeks burn. "Sorry, just got lost in my own head for a sec."

"Hey," he said softly. "It's okay that you like him. He's a good man."

She looked up and met Mr. Willis's kind brown eyes.

"I hear you lost your husband," he said. "I hope that's not forward of me to bring up."

"Not at all," she said. "And it's true. It was before we even found out about this one."

Her hand stroked her belly automatically.

"I can't think of a better man than Kellan Webb to treat that child like his own," Mr. Willis said. "Caring for folks is his whole life. But you better not sleep on it. His first wife might've left him, but he's considered a very eligible bachelor around here."

"I think I'm too late," she said miserably.

"Nah," Mr. Willis said, waving a hand in the air dismissively. "Girls like that are all smoke and mirrors, believe me, I've been around the block. Kellan deserves a woman of substance. One who believes in him and what he does—a partner."

Mr. Willis's words were kindly meant, but Daisy had seen enough of the world to know that she could not compete with the likes of the Aimees out there. That just wasn't how things worked.

"Thank you," she told him anyway, hoping her smile fooled him into believing she was feeling better.

"Are you kidding me?" Mr. Willis teased. "I should be thanking you. You're going to get me on Dr. Webb's VIP list, so I can call him at eight in the morning whenever I need a refill."

She laughed and applied herself to the task at hand, willing herself not to think about Kellan out with Aimee.

Of course, a man like Kellan doesn't want to be with a woman expecting another man's child, she told herself sternly. *A relationship with someone beautiful and sophisticated is exactly what he deserves. I should be happy for him. He's my friend, and that's enough. It's more than enough.*

23

DAISY

Daisy and Benny headed into the library together a few hours later.

Sure enough, Kellan hadn't reappeared before Benny got home, so Daisy closed up the office herself.

She was trying very hard not to picture him lingering over lunch with Aimee, making her laugh that husky laugh.

"I see the tree," Benny whispered excitedly, grabbing her hand.

"There are more people here than there were earlier," she told him quietly as she looked around the space that was now bustling with children and parents. "So, we're going to have to be really sneaky if we want to do this without anyone noticing."

"What do we do first?" Benny asked.

"Let's go over and look at the tree," she decided. "We'll look for the ornament with the biggest number on it, since we can afford to help a big family. Then when we know which one we want, it will be easier to slip over later and snag the ornament when no one is looking."

"Good thinking," Benny said, his eyes sparkling. "Grabbing the something without anyone noticing is a magician's trick - it's called sleight of hand."

"You can do it?" Daisy asked.

"Of course," Benny said, looking very pleased with himself.

"Perfect," she said. "When we get to that part, I'll stand guard and provide a distraction, like we did with that Santa."

"Daisy," a familiar voice said.

"Oh, hi, Holly," Daisy said, turning to see a familiar face. "It's so nice to see you here."

"Gotta get my weekly dose of YA Fantasy," Holly laughed.

Daisy had been stopping by the coffee shop where Holly was a waitress for hot tea and a cookie more often than she probably should have. She had struck up a conversation with Holly the first time she saw her immersed in a paperback behind the counter.

"Did they have the new Elfhame novel?" Daisy asked, knowing Holly had been waiting for it.

"I'm on the wait list," Holly said, shaking her head. "But I'm half tempted to go buy a copy from the bookshop, so I don't have to keep waiting. Hope you two find what you're looking for."

They waved their goodbyes and Holly headed out.

"She's nice," Benny said. "My dad wants me to eat healthy stuff, but she always brings me a little treat when we go to *Jolly Beans*."

"Your dad cares about you so much," Daisy said. "And you know what? His rabbit food isn't so bad once you get used to it."

"Rabbit food," Benny echoed in delight. "His *rabbit food*."

The nice librarian looked over at them in alarm.

"We'd better stay quiet, so we don't draw attention to ourselves," Daisy whispered to him.

Benny nodded and they made it the rest of the way to the tree in silence.

"Adopt a family for Christmas," Benny read out loud, then stopped suddenly, a worried look on his face.

"You don't like this idea?" she asked him.

"It's okay with me," he said bravely. "But will I have to share my room?"

She blinked at him for a moment and then it landed on her.

"I'm so sorry, Benny," she said, hoping she was doing a good job hiding her smile. "I should have explained. When you *adopt a family* for the holidays, it just means you buy them presents and help them, just like you would do for your own family. They don't actually come to live with you."

"Oh, that's good," Benny said. "Because I was pretty sure we should talk to my dad about it first if they were coming to live with us."

Daisy nodded in agreement, because she was pretty sure if she opened her mouth a giggle would come out.

They both scanned the tree. Most of the ornaments had a number two, three or four.

Benny pointed excitedly at one down near the bottom. It was partly tucked between two branches so that she couldn't see the number easily.

Daisy bent to look. It had a seven on it and the last name *Obersson*. She nodded to him, and he nodded back with sparkling eyes.

Looking around, she realized it was pretty quiet. She gestured to Benny to go ahead and snag the ornament.

Just then, Betty Ann Eustace came out of the Mystery section, nearly bumping into Daisy.

"Hello, there," Daisy said a little too loudly, hoping Benny would stop what he was doing.

"Well, hello, Daisy," Betty Ann said politely. "It's nice to see you supporting the local library with a visit."

"The library is free," Daisy blurted out without thinking.

"It's free for us, but did you know part of their funding is determined by how many visitors they receive?" Betty Ann asked.

"I didn't know that," Daisy said, feeling genuinely surprised.

"That's why the best thing we can do to support the library is use it," Betty Ann declared, hoisting a teetering stack of books onto the main counter.

"Well, if it isn't Benny Webb," a young woman called out, coming down the steps from the children's section.

"Hi, Miss Caroline," Benny said politely.

Daisy met his eye, and he gave his head a little shake.

So, he hadn't gotten the ornament. It would be up to her now.

"I just got in two new books on magicians," Miss Caroline told Benny. "And one is all about Houdini."

"Oh, wow," Benny said excitedly as they headed up the steps to the children's section. "Did you know that Harry Houdini could fly an airplane?"

Daisy waited until they were out of sight, then she took a quick sweep around.

No one was looking, so she grabbed the ornament and crammed it in her pocket before trotting up the steps after Benny and the children's librarian.

∼

ABOUT TWO HOURS LATER, they were leaving the mall, arms weighed down by at least a dozen shopping bags.

Daisy had even purchased a few items that weren't for the Obersson family, so that their trip to the mall would feel more normal to Kellan. Among those items were some cookie cutters in holiday shapes. She was hoping Benny might like to do some baking with her.

"I like the mall," Benny said as they piled their finds into Daisy's truck.

"Me too," she told him. "I love the decorations, and all the music playing. And I like to go from store to store without getting cold. But I think I like shopping in Trinity Falls even better."

"Me too," Benny said solemnly. "But we couldn't, if we wanted to keep a secret."

"Buying one or two things at a time in town is just fine," she told him. "But you're right. If we tried to buy all of this, someone could figure it out."

"I'm going to wrap the presents for the brother who is just a little bigger than me," Benny said excitedly.

"Yes, you are," Daisy agreed, feeling extra proud of Benny.

The boy in question had a special wishlist item. It was a Nintendo Switch, the exact handheld video gaming device that Benny really, really wanted, and his father wouldn't let him have.

When Benny saw Daisy point to it in the glass case, his eyes had gone wide.

She could see a touch of frustration on his face as he thought about finally buying that device just to give it to another boy.

"Can you imagine if you thought you weren't going to get any presents on Christmas and instead you unwrapped your present and saw that you got *this*?" Daisy asked him in a soft voice as the store worker handed it over. "He's going to be so grateful for this gift. And it's all because *you* chose his ornament."

The corners of Benny's mouth curved up into a smile.

"Did you guys adopt a family for Christmas?" the worker asked as he rang them up.

"We did," Benny said. "Look at all the stuff we got."

"That's amazing," the worker said, looking at all their bags. "Everyone on our block adopts a family for Christmas together each year. But we each only sign up for a few gifts. You guys are very generous."

"We're pretty lucky, and grateful for the opportunity to pay it forward," Daisy said. "Right, Benny?"

"It's really fun," Benny said, nodding his head up and down. "We picked a family with seven people, and I'm seven years old."

"Merry Christmas," the cashier had said, with a big smile for Benny.

They loaded up the truck and drove home in happy silence. Flurries were falling again, but Daisy was grateful that they weren't sticking yet.

But maybe the luckiest thing to happen was that Kellan wasn't there when they pulled up.

"Wow, your dad's having a nice long lunch," Daisy said with a bravado she didn't feel.

"It's almost dinner," Benny pointed out.

"Well, let's get this stuff inside, since no one is here to see it," Daisy said. "Maybe we can get some wrapping done before your dad gets back."

"Can we do it in my room and listen to music?" Benny asked. "Grandpa got me a radio."

"Sure," she told him.

They brought the gifts and wrapping paper back to his room and put on the radio.

Bobby Helms was singing *Jingle Bell Rock,* and Daisy couldn't resist tapping her foot along to the beat as they carefully removed all the price tags and began wrapping gifts.

Each time they finished one person's gifts, Daisy dashed downstairs to stash the presents in her closet. By the time they had most of the family members squared away, the two of them were laughing and singing along with the radio.

Daisy put a bow on top of Benny's head, and then he put one on hers.

She noticed that Benny seemed to be saving the little boy's gifts for last, she assumed so that he could have a little more time before saying goodbye to the handheld game.

It wasn't hurting anyone, so she obligingly kept working on whatever he chose to wrap next.

They were almost finished, with only the gaming device left to go when she heard an engine pulling up out front.

"Oh, let me go hide these in my closet," Daisy said.

"Can I just look at this for one more minute?" Benny asked.

"Sure," Daisy said. "But as soon as I come back, you'll have to surrender it."

He laughed and turned the box over to read the description on the back.

She dashed off with everything else, ready to tuck it quickly into her closet.

All the gifts took up so much space that she had to remove her backpack and toss it onto her bed before fitting everything in.

The closet door managed to close perfectly, with all the gifts hidden.

She let out a sigh of relief and headed out of her room to join Benny. They could just tuck the last gift into one of the drawers in his dresser to wrap later.

But she heard the front door close before she could get back upstairs.

It's okay, she told herself. *Benny heard that, too. He'll hide the box someplace safe.*

Daisy headed out to the truck to grab the bag of everyday items she had purchased, feeling a little off balance, though she couldn't explain why.

24

KELLAN

K ellan jogged up the stairs to see how Benny was doing.

Though he knew that very few parents were with their children every single moment they weren't in school, Benny was used to having him home and ready to listen to his joys and sorrows and funny stories about school.

Since he was Benny's only parent most of the time, Kellan was determined to be there as much as possible. And he felt bad about getting home so late.

Benny's door was open, and he was sitting on his bed by himself, holding something and looking at it intently.

"Hey, buddy," Kellan said, causing Benny to jump.

A guilty look appeared on his little face, and he tried to put what he was holding under his pillow.

That wasn't normal behavior for him.

And where was Daisy? Kellan had expected the two to be practically joined at the hip, as usual.

"What have you got there?" Kellan asked gently, sitting beside him on the bed.

Benny opened his mouth and closed it again, and then held out the object in question.

Kellan didn't recognize what it was at first. He held the little box in his hands and flipped it over.

The image on the front of the box made it clear what was inside.

"The Switch," he said, feeling fury rise in his chest. "Did your mother get this for you?"

Benny shook his head and didn't meet his father's eyes.

"I'm waiting," Kellan said. "Where did this come from? I know your grandparents didn't get it for you."

His parents would have fallen over just at the knowledge of how much this little thing cost. If they were aware of the violence in the mindless games that flashed on its addictive screen, they would be exponentially more upset.

"It's not mine," Benny said softly.

Kellan blinked at him.

Benny was a regular little boy. He had moments where he lost his temper or cried. He had even stomped his foot and talked back a time or two, usually when he was tired and stressed, or Kellan hadn't fed him soon enough.

But Benny wasn't a liar.

"I'm going to ask you one more time," Kellan said in the calmest voice he was capable of. "And you're going to tell me the truth. Who bought this Switch?"

"*Daisy*," Benny whispered miserably.

Another lie. Daisy didn't have the money for something this expensive. And even if she did, she would never buy Benny a present like this without asking Kellan's permission.

It hit him again that he really hadn't known her for long.

"Daisy bought this?" he demanded, looking directly into his son's eyes.

Benny nodded, never breaking eye contact.

He was telling the truth.

Kellan was up in a heartbeat, ready to have a serious talk with Daisy. How dare she buy something for Benny that Kellan didn't want him to have?

"Please don't make her go away," Benny blurted out suddenly.

Kellan stopped in the threshold and turned to see tears flying down Benny's cheeks.

"Daisy is an adult," Kellan said. "And you're my child. When I trust her with you, and she does something inappropriate, like buying you an extremely expensive gift for a much older child, without talking to me about it, the right thing for me to do is talk to her."

Benny only cried harder.

"Son, I'm disappointed that you didn't ask her not to buy it, knowing that I don't want you having it," Kellan told him a little more gently. "But you're just a kid. She's supposed to be the adult."

He headed down the stairs, feeling angrier than ever. Benny was so upset. He hadn't seen the boy like that in... well, ever.

Kellan stalked through the kitchen and back to Daisy's room, thinking up exactly what he was going to say to her about the game system.

"Daisy," he said sternly as he approached her open door.

But when he stepped inside, she wasn't there.

And when he saw what was on her bed, his jaw dropped.

A beat-up looking backpack sat on her pillow, the main compartment open. And a dozen packets of cash, each one at least an inch thick and marked *$2,000.00*, spilled out onto the flowered comforter of Kellan's guest room.

"Kellan," Daisy's voice sounded upbeat and happy as she

headed down the hall to him. "Benny and I had so much fun at the mall."

Kellan felt a coldness fall over him that was beyond anger.

25

DAISY

Daisy approached her room, trepidation bubbling up in her chest.

Kellan was standing there, not turning, not responding to her.

"Kellan?" she repeated softly as she reached the doorway.

He stepped aside.

Her breath caught in her throat when she saw what he had been looking at. Her backpack was open on the bed, and her cursed fortune was spilling out onto the covers.

"What is this?" Kellan asked without moving.

His voice wasn't angry. It was flat, emotionless.

"I-I..." Daisy searched for the words. She wasn't even sure where to begin explaining. "Kellan—"

"You know what?" he said, turning to her abruptly. "I don't want to know. I've already made a fool of myself. I don't want to be complicit in whatever is going on here."

"Complicit?" she echoed, completely confused.

"I'm an idiot," Kellan said flatly. "I let you into my home. I allowed you to develop a relationship with my son. And all this time, I thought you were a sweet, innocent young girl, trying to make the best of a bad situation. I thought I was helping you, not letting you drag my family down with you—"

"I'm not a sweet, innocent young *anything*," she heard herself spit. "I'm a grown woman who is about to become a mother. And I'm not dragging anyone down. You know what? You've lived a charmed life, Kellan Webb, and it shows."

She scooped the cash back into her backpack, for the first time feeling that it wasn't cursed at all. It was a resource she was using to help people.

She grabbed her clothing out of the single drawer it took up and shoved that in there too, then turned to Kellan.

"It'll be a cold day in H-E-double hockey sticks when I let the judgement of a self-important stick-in-the-mud like you reflect on *my* self-worth," she said crisply before she turned on her heel and marched out.

She made it out the front door, down the steps and onto the sidewalk before the tears began to stream down her face.

Resolute, she kept walking, determined that if he looked out the window, he wouldn't have the satisfaction of seeing her try to wipe away her tears.

It was so cold outside, and she probably should have gotten into her truck and driven away.

But she honestly had no idea where to go. And besides, something seemed to be moving her feet, urging her down the sidewalk toward the village.

"I'm so sorry, baby," she said, wrapping an arm around her belly. "I lost us a warm home and a steady job. But don't you worry. I'll turn this around, and we'll wind up even better off than we were before. You'll see."

Somehow, her assurances to the baby made her feel

better about everything herself. After all, she would never let her daughter down, not ever. She knew to her bones that she would do whatever it took to give them both a safe and happy life.

She marched on, past the Co-op and the little shops along Columbia, and made a right onto Park, taking deep, cleansing breaths of the crisp air.

The Christmas lights in the windows of the storefronts looked so cozy, especially from outside in the blue darkness.

Up ahead, on the corner by the train station, she could see that *Jolly Beans* was open, but there were almost no customers inside. On a whim, she decided to stop in and treat herself to a hot chocolate and a good think.

She was standing outside, trying to wipe away all evidence of her crying when the door swung open, and Holly Fields stepped out in her coat with her purse over her shoulder.

"Daisy, are you okay?" Holly asked, her own face falling.

"I'll be fine," Daisy told her. "Your shift is over. I'll bet you're just about asleep on your feet."

"No, no, no," Holly said, smiling as she scolded Daisy. "Young lady, you're going to march in there and tell me everything."

Daisy knew she should say no, but it was impossible to resist the comfort of talking with a friend.

"Really?" she asked.

"Oh, definitely," Holly told her.

"Then I'm buying," Daisy said. "So, I hope you're hungry."

Holly's face broke into a grin, and she turned and held the door open for Daisy. Together, they headed to the table up in the big front window.

"What are you doing here?" Pete asked Holly. He winked to show he was kidding.

"Meatloaf sandwich, please," Holly said with an ecstatic smile. "And a gingerbread latte."

"And for you, ma'am?" Pete asked Daisy.

"I had a whole thing planned," Daisy laughed. "But after hearing her order, I just want the same."

"Two meatloaf sandwiches, two gingerbread lattes," Pete said with a smile. "Coming right up."

"So, what's going on?" Holly asked.

"It's complicated, maybe even boring," Daisy said. "But the long and short of it is that I left Kellan's place, and now I'm without a job *and* without a home."

"Why?" Holly breathed, her blue eyes wide with horror. "I thought he was in love with you. He's a good man, Daisy, even if he is a little on the serious side."

Her heart tried to surge, and then she remembered Aimee.

"He's not in love with me," Daisy said flatly. "He's seeing someone. But that's not really what it's all about. He doesn't trust me. And I can't be in an environment like that, especially now."

Her hand had moved to cradle her belly once more.

Holly nodded and patted Daisy's other hand.

It was a warm gesture that had the tears prickling Daisy's eyes again.

"So, do you want possible solutions, or just sympathy?" Holly asked.

"Both, please," Daisy said, laughing even though her eyes were wet again.

"I know it's a far cry from using your nursing certificate," Holly said. "But just for now, would you want to work here? Pete's down a server, one of the college kids has mono. It might be fun to work together, for a little while at least."

"That would be amazing," Daisy said. "Do you think he'd hire me though?"

"Oh, everyone knows what a doll you are," Holly said. "He'd be a fool not to. Hey, Pete."

"Yeah?" Pete asked from behind the counter where he was fixing their lattes.

"Can Daisy fill in for Erika for a bit?" Holly asked. "She's between gigs right now."

"You have any experience, Daisy?" Pete asked.

"Sorry," she said sadly. "I've never worked in a restaurant before."

"Perfect," Pete said, perking up. "No bad habits to break. When can you start?"

But Daisy's phone had started ringing.

"Dr. Webb," Holly said knowingly.

But Daisy didn't recognize the number.

"Hello?" she said.

"Daisy?" a woman's voice asked. "It's Sloane, from Trinity Falls Realty Group. Are you still looking for a place to live?"

"I am," Daisy said.

"Well, it's only temporary," Sloane said. "But Professor Mickelwaite is on sabbatical in Portugal with his whole family for six months. They've only been gone a week and their housesitter had to bow out to be with her mother in Missouri. They're desperate for someone who can move right in and keep an eye on the place. Of course, I thought of you right away. Are you interested?"

"Oh, my goodness," Daisy said. "Are you kidding me? I'd be honored."

"Wonderful," Sloane told her. "You'll also be paid. It's not much, but maybe a little something to add to your moving fund for when the Mickelwaites come back. The house is on Oberlin. If you'd like, you can come see it now."

Holly was gazing at Daisy with a question on her face.

And Sloane was waiting for an answer.

But for just a second, Daisy allowed herself to close her eyes and say a silent prayer of thanksgiving.

"Daisy?" Sloane said.

"Sorry about that," Daisy said. "Yes, of course, I'll meet you there. I can't believe there's an opportunity to housesit right here in Trinity Falls."

She and Sloane signed off.

"Better make all that food to go, Pete," Holly called to him. "It looks like our friend Daisy's guardian angel is working overtime tonight."

26

KELLAN

Kellan paced the floors, running a hand through his hair and trying to figure out what to do next.

He was beside himself with worry. The flurries outside were turning to snow, and Daisy had left on foot. Her truck was still out front.

No matter what she had done, it wasn't right for her to be out there, wandering around in the dark and the cold, especially in her condition.

And especially not with all that cash on her.

His mind went back to the news headline he'd seen when he searched Quail Creek:

$25,000 of Opioids Missing in Suspected Robbery at Quail Creek Clinic.

It was impossible to believe, but it was the simplest explanation. Daisy was a nurse, who might very well have worked at that clinic. And he had seen the amount of cash on her bed.

Sure, it was possible that she had come by that cash

honestly. But nothing about the way she presented herself suggested that she was wealthy.

Besides, most people didn't carry around that kind of cash, no matter how well off they were. The only reason to carry that much cash was if you didn't want to put the money in the bank for some reason.

And not wanting a paper trail suggested guilt.

But that didn't matter right now. Even if she had done something wrong, there was no reason for him to have chased her out into the snow.

He had told her he was her friend, but a real friend would have talked to her, and tried to help her see that she needed to make things right.

She's in a bad position, expecting a baby, with no one in the world but herself to provide for it. Maybe she thought stealing and selling those drugs was her only option.

She had a good heart. That was his first instinct about her the night they met, and he knew it now more than ever.

Drowning in guilt, he pulled his phone out of his pocket and tried calling her again, but it went straight to voicemail, like the last dozen times.

He had tried talking to Benny when he wasn't able to reach Daisy the first time.

But Benny had buttoned his lips.

"Daisy is my friend," he told his father. "I promised her I wouldn't talk about the Switch, and I won't."

"I'm your father," Kellan had tried to reason. "You can't keep secrets from your grown-ups."

"It's not that kind of secret," Benny had said, incomprehensibly.

Kellan blinked at him.

"You can punish me if you need to," Benny added bravely. "I understand."

But in the face of such dedicated loyalty to a friend, a friend who Kellan himself had abandoned when she needed him most, he didn't have the heart to dole out a punishment.

Instead, he had pulled his son into a hug.

"Is Daisy okay?" Benny whispered. "Why did she leave?"

"We'll make sure she's okay," Kellan had told him.

But now he wasn't sure how he could do that.

Glancing at his watch, he saw that it was just after nine at night. She had been gone less than two hours, though it felt like a lifetime to him. He couldn't exactly call her a missing person.

And much as he wanted to go out after her himself, Benny was now asleep upstairs, and Kellan couldn't leave him alone.

He opened the front door and stepped out onto the porch.

The wind had picked up. It was swirling the dust of flurries that had gathered on the sidewalks, making the whole street look almost like it was floating on a cloud.

He shivered, but stayed where he was, looking as far as he could in every direction, wishing he could scream her name into the night without waking half the block.

If I don't hear from her by ten, I'll call Cal Cassidy, he told himself. *He can't file a missing person's report, but he'll ask his guys to keep a look out for her, maybe even send a patrol car around.*

Kellan sat on one of the wooden rocking chairs out on the porch, rubbing his hands together for warmth.

If she was out there in the cold somewhere, he could good and well be outdoors himself.

27

DAISY

When they got to the house, Daisy let Sloane go inside before her as she stood out on the front walk, looking up at the Mickelwaites' old Victorian home on Oberlin Avenue.

It was a pale gray with white trim and black shutters. And though the Mickelwaites hadn't even planned to be here for the holidays, strings of Christmas lights were hung around the porch and eaves.

With the flurries falling, it looked like a classic holiday house in a snow globe.

One by one, the windows lit up, until the whole house glowed warmly.

She smiled at the idea that Sloane was turning the lights on for her, as if she needed to be convinced to accept the miracle that was in front of her.

Daisy would have been weak with relief at the chance to live in a shack, or rent a room on the edge of town. This was... excessively wonderful.

Even if I don't deserve it, you do, she thought, patting her belly. *There's no reason you shouldn't have every blessing in the world.*

Sloane came out to the porch again, slightly breathless from the trek up and down all those stairs.

"Hey," she said with a smile. "I just wanted to get all the lights on, so you could see how nice it is."

"Thank you," Daisy told her. "I'm grateful at the chance to have a place to live at all. But this looks as pretty as a doll-house—such a magical place for a little girl to be welcomed into the world."

Sloane beamed down at her, and Daisy grabbed the handrail and climbed the steps to the front porch, ready to go see what the next half-year of her life was going to look like.

An hour later, Sloane was pulling her car out of the driveway as Daisy waved goodbye from the porch.

Daisy had the keys, and a written rundown of the trash and recycling schedule, as well as instructions on who to call if there were any issues with plumbing, electrical, roofing or yard work.

"Okay, first thing we need to do is turn all these lights off," she said out loud to the baby. "We don't want to run up Professor Mickelwaite's bills."

She closed the front door and walked through the house a second time, admiring the lovely rooms. Though it wasn't modern or fancy, it was neat and tidy. And she felt like she was getting to know the owners just by admiring their family photos on the walls, and the books spilling off the built-in shelves that seemed to grace nearly every single room.

When she had turned out the lights on all three floors of

the old house, she came back to the kitchen with its leafy wallpaper and wooden cupboards.

There were tins of herbal tea on the counter and an electric kettle was set beside the sink. She decided to start some water boiling, so she would have a hot cup of tea when she had done the thing she was dreading doing.

As the water filled the kettle, she tried to steady her breath.

You've known them such a short time, she reminded herself. *This shouldn't be so hard.*

When the kettle was going, she pulled her phone out of her pocket and powered it up.

She'd turned it off, since Kellan's calls had been stressing her out earlier, but she knew she had to communicate with him, even if he was furious with her. It was the right thing to do.

The screen lit up and she saw over twenty missed calls and a string of message notifications with the last name *Webb.*

She ignored them all, and tapped on his contact instead. There was no point looking at angry messages. It would be easier to just face the music.

His phone rang once and then she heard his voice.

"Daisy?" he practically shouted.

"Kellan, listen," she said. "I know you're angry. I just wanted to let you know that I've found a place to stay, and I'll be back tomorrow for the rest of my stuff and my truck. I'll come by while you're working, and I'll leave your key on the counter and lock the door behind me."

"Daisy—" he tried to break in again, the excess emotion coming through in his voice. He clearly hadn't cooled down yet, which meant he must have been even angrier than she thought.

"Amy Jo and Todd Bradford were planning to come in tomorrow afternoon for me to show them the portal," she went on crisply. "You may want to get in touch with them if you aren't available to do it yourself."

"You don't have to quit—" he began.

"I have another job, and a new place to live," she said firmly.

"How?" he asked, his tone awed.

"I guess I have a couple of guardian angels," she said lightly. "Please tell Benny I said goodbye."

But her voice caught on the last word, and she couldn't say more without sobbing at the idea of not seeing the sweet little boy again.

"Daisy, wait—" Kellan said.

But she hung up as fast as she could, knowing that prolonging the inevitable wouldn't do her any good.

Once the phone was back in her pocket, she let the tears fall while she fixed her mug of tea. Even the scent of the chamomile made her think of Kellan.

Then she headed up to Professor Mickelwaite's daughter's pink bedroom with her tea and her few belongings.

Sloane had said that Daisy could spread out in the primary suite, but she felt much more comfortable curled up on little Janey's bed, surrounded by all the soft stuffed animals and colorful picture books that she thought her own little one might like to have one day.

Although she had been the recipient of not just one but *two* miracles tonight, she still found it hard to think about anything but Benny and Kellan as she tried hopelessly to sleep.

Maybe one day, he'll change his mind about me, she told herself. *Maybe one day, he'll be calm enough for me to explain.*

But she knew that was only wishful thinking. Clearly,

Benny would already have told his father exactly what she was doing with the money, and why he had the game system.

And Kellan was still furious with her. She'd heard his voice practically trembling with rage.

We don't need them, she told the baby in her mind. *We are enough, just the two of us.*

If only she could convince her aching heart that it was true.

DAISY

Daisy set down a pair of peppermint mochas on a table in front of two young moms who were chatting away.

"Thank you," one of them stopped to say, squinting at her name tag. "Daisy."

"You're welcome," Daisy said, turning to grab the next table's order.

"Hey, wait," the other one said. "Are you Daisy Mullen?"

"That's me," she said, surprised.

"I figured there couldn't be too many new faces in town with the name Daisy," the other woman said with a warm smile. "You helped my parents get set up on Dr. Webb's new computer system."

"Small world," Daisy said, smiling back.

"Is Dr. Webb not paying you enough?" the other woman asked, a furrow in her forehead.

Daisy blinked at her for a minute, then put two and two together.

"Oh goodness no. He was very generous," she said. "But

I'm not working there anymore. That was just a temporary position to get folks used to the new system."

"Get out of town," the second lady said, shaking her head. "He's a fool to let you go. My parents said you were the only thing standing between them and the twenty-four-hour clinic up on Route One. The personal touch at Dr. Wilkinson's office is the thing that kept them coming back all those years."

"I'm sure he'll hire a new receptionist soon," Daisy said. "I need to run drinks to another table, but it was very nice to meet you."

As she rushed off to grab a green juice and a gingerbread latte for the window table, she wondered if the lady had been right.

As upset as she was about him ditching her, she wanted nothing but the best for Kellan. It would be a real shame if he lost his patients to that new clinic when he was such a wonderful doctor and he clearly cared so much.

Luckily, things were too busy for her to worry for long. Table after table filled up, ate, tipped, and emptied again, as Christmas music played on the radio.

The café even smelled like the holidays, with Pete's special cranberry bread baking, and hundreds of peppermint mochas and gingerbread lattes being prepared and doled out.

It was so much fun to work with Holly, too. The perky blonde was so upbeat and quick, and their rhythms seemed to match up well. Of course, Holly was a much more experienced waitress than Daisy, but she offered her plenty of help and advice.

They had even started a fun rivalry over the last few days. They would choose a menu item together each morning, and each of them would mention it to customers, hoping they would decide to order it. Whoever sold the most of the item in question bought lunch for the other. Since they got a generous employee discount, it wasn't too risky a game.

Today's secret challenge item was the Yuletide Shake - an eggnog ice cream shake with cinnamon syrup and a sprinkle of baking spices on the whipped cream topping.

Poor Anton, the community college student who was working the counter, kept groaning every time one of them put in another Yuletide Shake order.

"Why are so many people ordering milkshakes before nine in the morning?" he asked plaintively. "This is seriously weird, guys."

Daisy almost felt sorry for him for having to prepare all those shakes and clean the blender every time.

But Holly only laughed and winked at her.

She and Holly shared their tips with the counter staff, even though they sat on a stool behind the counter while she and Holly ran all over the café dealing with customers. She figured Holly was trying to tell her it was okay to make him earn it.

She smiled back at her new friend, and headed off to another table to get their food order.

Her life was starting to feel like her own again. The job was exhausting, especially so late in her pregnancy. But people were extra generous with tips, and she loved working with Holly and with the mostly lively, friendly customers. The café was warm and fragrant. And Pete was lavish with his praise when she had a good day.

The big house on Oberlin felt more like home every time she walked up to it. But it still felt empty at night, and she walked the long way down Park Avenue to Princeton and then back up Oberlin to avoid Kellan's place on Columbia Avenue.

It was working out so far, but she was finding it much harder to avoid the Webb boys in her thoughts than on her walks.

When she had grabbed her stuff from the house, including the presents in the closet, she had noticed that Kellan had left the Nintendo Switch on her bed. She'd had to wrap that one on her own.

It was bittersweet to drop off the gifts for their adopted family without Benny. But she hoped he knew she was taking care of it.

Now, each time she shoved a little more of the cash into a donation can, or bought a secret gift for someone, she thought of Benny, and how much more meaningful it was to share the joy of giving with him.

She'd actually started hearing some buzz about the Trinity Falls Secret Santa, so some of her good deeds were definitely getting noticed. She only hoped she could keep up the secret part.

Happily, she was having more thoughts every day about the arrival of her own little one, who was more active than ever, especially when Daisy sat down at the end of the day.

She wasn't due for another month, but she had already purchased a few things like a crib, car seat, and stroller.

"I have to run to the post office," Holly told her later that afternoon. "Need anything from town?"

"I'm good," Daisy told her.

"Gosh, I love this coat," Holly said, snuggling into the faux fur lining around the hood. "So wild that I have a secret admirer. But honestly, who could blame them?"

"The Trinity Falls Secret Santa strikes again," Pete yelled from behind the counter.

"He can be Santa *and* an admirer," Holly called back.

Daisy just smiled and watched after her friend.

She had noticed a few days ago that Holly was coming in holding her old coat closed with her hand because the zipper had broken.

Unlike Daisy, Holly didn't have a place to live that paid her just to be there, and though she didn't talk about it, it seemed like she might have been using her money to help out family. Daisy figured maybe things were too tight for Holly to splurge on something for herself, even something as important as a jacket in a Pennsylvania winter.

So, Daisy had carefully chosen the pretty blue coat to match Holly's eyes, then waited for a day when Holly was scheduled to open, and set it on one of the metal café tables outside *Jolly Beans* in a box with Holly's name on it.

The note hadn't said it was from a secret admirer, but she loved that Holly took it just that way. And Daisy *did* admire Holly, although it wasn't a secret. She would always be grateful to her new friend for taking her under her wing.

Three Yuletide shakes later, Holly was back from the post office, and the sun was setting outside. Normally, the traffic slowed a little around now, but everyone must have been out shopping for Christmas. The tables were filled with happy customers, with bags and bundles draped over the backs of chairs and stuffed under the tables.

The bell over the door rang and Daisy looked over automatically and nearly did a double take.

Kellan Webb was standing in the doorway, dressed in a button-down shirt and a pair of jeans, and looking sinfully gorgeous.

She tore her eyes away, but not before he caught her looking.

"Daisy," he said.

"Holly can get you whatever you need," she told him, turning to hurry away.

"I don't think she can," he said, a little louder. "Because what I need is to talk to you."

Customers began turning around to look.

"Can we please step outside for a moment?" he asked her, his beautiful blue eyes pleading.

"Anything you have to say to me you can say right here," she told him firmly.

29

KELLAN

K ellan stood in the doorway of *Jolly Beans* café, realizing he had never been so afraid in his life.

He hadn't been this scared as a child in the haunted house at the Trinity Falls Halloween Hop, or as a teen jumping from the cliffside into Trinity Lake on a dare. He hadn't even been this worried when his hands shook and his heart pounded a mile a minute as he took his medical boards.

But Daisy Mullen was important to him, and she was important to Benny, too. This time apart had shown him that she was the missing piece of the puzzle that was their family, and the glue that was holding his medical practice together as well. There was no facet of his life she hadn't touched and made infinitely better in their short time together.

And as nervous as he might be to declare himself in public, he was much, much more scared that he might lose her forever. Or that maybe he already had.

And that would be unforgivable.

"I'm sorry," he heard himself say in a deep, steady voice.

"I was an idiot to let you leave, and I have regretted it every minute of every day since then."

As one, every face in the coffee shop turned to Daisy to see what she would say.

"Don't worry about it," she said.

"I care about you, Daisy Mullen," he said, his voice breaking a little on her name. "You mean everything to me. And to Benny, too. You make every part of our lives happier and better."

"I care about you, too," she said, her face softening a little. "But you're seeing someone. And I think my feelings for you are a little too complicated for us to try to be friends again right now."

All eyes were back on him again now.

"Seeing someone?" he echoed stupidly.

"Aimee?" she said, her eyebrows raised like she thought he was being deliberately obtuse.

"Aimee?" he echoed again. "Oh. Oh wow."

"*Oh wow*," she said, shaking her head and rolling her eyes. "You *forgot* your girlfriend?"

"She's not—" he started.

"See, this is why we can't be friends—" she began.

"Daisy, she's *not* my girlfriend," he broke in.

"She's—she's not?" she asked, blinking at him like she had lost her whole train of thought.

There were murmurs of surprise in the café.

"No," he said. "Of course not. She's a very nice person, but she's not my type. Aimee is a pharmaceutical sales rep. I don't let reps influence what I prescribe. But if I go to lunch with her every month, she's allowed to give me unlimited free samples, and those are very helpful for my patients."

He didn't exactly want to yell out in front of the whole

town that times were tight and many of his patients relied on the free meds, but he hoped she understood.

She nodded, her face thoughtful now.

"Have dinner with me, so I can apologize better," he said, taking a step closer. "Please."

Two ladies at a booth in the corner let out audible sighs, and a woman at one of the tables between him and where Daisy stood quietly slid two of her bags off the back of her chair and under the table, as if to make room for him to get to her.

But Daisy stepped back, her dark eyes still solemn.

"I'll think about it," she said after a moment.

It's not a no.

"Yes," he said, feeling so happy he could fly. "Yes, please think about it. That's all I'm asking. You know where to find me. I'll wait for you, Daisy, as long as it takes."

She nodded once.

Maybe it was wishful thinking, but he swore the corners of her mouth were curving up very slightly as she turned on her heel and marched off to talk to a customer.

"Good job, son," one of the old Williams brothers whispered to him as he passed, smacking his arm approvingly. "Sometimes you've just gotta tell 'em how you feel."

"I guess we'll see," Kellan said. "Sure hope you're right."

"Course you do," the old man cackled. "Look at her. She's the sweetest little thing in the world, and not bad to look at either."

Kellan chuckled and headed back out into the cold twilight.

The air tasted like snow. A storm was on the way.

But he didn't care.

For the first time in all the dark nights since Daisy left, Kellan Webb had hope in his heart.

30

DAISY

Daisy stood in the kitchen that evening, cradling a mug of tea in her hands as she gazed out the window and thought about everything Kellan had said.

Outside, the snow was falling thick and fast, like something out of a movie. But here in the Mickelwaite kitchen, she was snug and warm.

"We're right where we're supposed to be," she told the baby.

Her belly tightened as if in response, and this time it hurt a little.

Ever since she finished her work shift, she had been having these feelings. Since the baby wasn't due for a month, she figured they were Braxton Hicks contractions—the practice kind that many women experienced in the month or so before childbirth.

"Almost time," she told the baby as she began to walk around the first floor, hoping it would ease the sensation of a band around her belly. "A few more weeks, sweet girl."

She passed a family portrait of the Mickelwaites as she

walked down the hall. It must have been taken at a big family reunion in the seventies. There were boys in sweater vests with hair to their shoulders, and women in cute dresses with knee socks. Their happiness was palpable.

Kellan's words echoed in her head again.

I care about you, Daisy Mullen. You mean everything to me. And to Benny, too. You make every part of our lives happier and better.

Could they be like the people in that photo one day, if she opened her heart? Four faces in a sea of generations, finding comfort and happiness in each other through thick and thin?

She kept walking, breathing easier now that her belly had relaxed.

There were embroidered throw pillows on the living room sofa. Some were adorned with flowers or houses, others were emblazoned with cute sayings, like *Bless this Mess* and *Theatre is My Sport.* One in particular caught her eye tonight.

To err is human, to forgive divine.

Was that a lesson meant for her?

Kellan had kicked her out, and insulted her honor as well. He had seen that money, and assumed that she was some kind of criminal.

But somehow, she didn't feel as hurt or angry tonight.

After all, what was he supposed to think? Normal people didn't walk around with tens of thousands of dollars in a beat-up backpack.

Her belly tightened again, and this time there was real pain.

She hissed in a breath and leaned against the mantel. Were Braxton Hicks contractions supposed to feel like this?

When the band of fire let her go this time, she moved more slowly afterward as she got back into her train of thought.

If Kellan was right to be concerned about the cash in her bag and the video game, then why was she so angry at him?

It hurt at the time that he hadn't given her a chance to explain. But would she have acted any differently if someone she trusted with her child appeared to be in the middle of something shady?

This is about me, too, she realized. *It's not all about him.*

She continued through the house, feeling the pieces begin to fit together.

All this time, she had been furious, feeling as though he was treating her like a worthless girl from Quail Creek.

But he wasn't really doing that.

No one in Trinity Falls had treated her that way. Everyone here treated her with genuine kindness and respect.

The only one hung up on where I'm from is me.

That realization was enough to stop her in her tracks.

All her positive thinking didn't matter a bit, if somewhere in the back of her head she actually thought of herself as the kind of worthless human her old landlord could push around.

You can take the girl out of Quail Creek, but you can't take Quail Creek out of the girl, Al would have rasped, laughing at his own joke.

But in a way he was right. If she couldn't get rid of this chip on her shoulder, and accept that she was worth as much as anyone else in the world, she was going to keep sabotaging her own happiness.

That was a very sad thought on its own.

And she was about to become a mother.

"I'm going to do better, baby," she whispered to her daughter, rubbing a hand around her belly. "We're worth it."

She was going to forgive Kellan, and she was going to let him take her out for dinner.

She was going to accept the happiness the universe had seen fit to offer her and her daughter, filling their lives with a man and a wonderful little boy.

And she wasn't going to question whether she was worthy of any it, not ever again.

Suddenly, she couldn't wait to talk to Kellan again.

It was after Benny's bedtime, but this was too important for a phone call anyway. She decided she would go to Kellan tomorrow. Maybe she could catch him before her shift started, and they could talk in person.

Her belly tightened again. This time the pain was enough to take her breath away.

She clung to the wall and closed her eyes.

This was not practice.

I'm in labor, she realized. *This is it.*

Her heart pounded with joy and fear. The baby was early, but only by a few weeks. She just had to get herself to the hospital.

When the contraction released her, she rushed to the door and grabbed her keys. Slipping on her coat, she headed out into the snow.

It was coming down hard and fast. This was no flurry or dusting. It was a real storm. She stood on the sidewalk, debating calling an ambulance. It probably wasn't the best idea to drive, but she couldn't imagine the cost of an ambulance. And it was such a short trip to the hospital up on Route One.

Pain seared across her abdomen, and she felt hot liquid release between her legs.

Her nurse's mind told her what she should have been paying attention to all along.

It had been far less than five minutes since the last contraction.

I'm not going to make it to the hospital.

31

KELLAN

Kellan couldn't sleep.

He didn't want to admit to himself that he was waiting for Daisy's call, but that was exactly what he was doing.

Here he was, at the end of a long day, with Benny finally asleep, with the snow falling hard outside. And instead of getting his rest in his warm bed, he was pacing the living room, probably walking the finish off the wood floor between the Christmas tree and the dining room doorway, waiting for her to call.

She's not going to call tonight, a little voice in the back of his head told him. *Her day starts early, too.*

But something kept him walking.

It had been a little wild going to her at work today, and throwing himself on her mercy with what had felt like half the town watching.

They'd have a hard time teasing him for being dead serious all the time now. He'd made a complete fool of himself for love in front of everyone.

But instead of thinking about his friends and neighbors

chuckling at him, all he could think about was the slight curve of her lips as he was leaving.

Does that mean she'll come back to me? Will she give me a chance?

A sudden knock at the front door roused him and he ran to answer it, hoping against hope.

When he opened the door to find Daisy outside in the swirling snow he paused for a moment.

It almost felt like she was a figment of his imagination, like he had conjured the illusion of her from his prayers.

"Daisy?" he murmured.

"Kellan," she said brokenly, her voice wonderfully, beautifully real.

"What are you doing out there in the snowstorm?" he asked her, pulling her inside. "It's dangerous out there."

"I'm s-sorry to bother you," she whimpered. "If it's not too much trouble—"

But whatever she was going to say next was cut off as she practically collapsed in his arms, her whole body rippling as she clutched him, moaning with agony.

"The baby is coming," he realized out loud.

Terror filled his chest. It wasn't her time yet. And it was snowing too hard to get her to the hospital where they had all the equipment and assistance needed for an early birth.

Then his professional cool kicked in, and he was able to momentarily set aside that this was the woman he loved, and dedicate himself to caring for her.

"I've got you," he assured her. "I'm going to hold you through this one. Then we'll walk you back to your bed and get you comfortable."

He could actually *feel* her relax at the sound of his voice.

At last, the contraction subsided. But before he could get her to her room, he heard footsteps on the stairs.

"Dad?" Benny called down in a sleepy voice.

He would have called back for the boy not to come down, but it was too late, he had reached the last few steps and he saw who was there.

"Daisy," he cried ecstatically, launching himself down the last two steps and into her arms.

"Easy, Benny," Kellan said. "Daisy is going to have her baby tonight, so we have to get her back to her room and make her nice and cozy."

"You're having your baby?" Benny asked her with a huge smile. "You're so excited to meet her."

"I am," she said. And in spite of her fear and exhaustion, warmth radiated from her when she spoke with his son.

"We should go to your room, Daisy," Benny told her, taking her hand. "You should lie down in your nice bed."

"Your quilt," she said worriedly, turning back to Kellan.

His mother had made the beautiful quilt that was on the bed in the guest room.

"Oh, that's not a problem at all," he told her. "Benny, go get the nice big fluffy comforter from my bed, and the soft fluffy blanket from your chair in your room."

Benny took off like a shot, and Kellan led Daisy back toward her room.

But they didn't make it all the way back before she was moaning again.

"Hold onto me," he told her. "Squeeze me as hard as you need to."

"Daisy?" Benny asked worriedly as he ran back to them with the fluffy blanket around his shoulders and the comforter dragging behind him.

"She's okay. But it's very hard work for Daisy to get the baby out," Kellan told him carefully. "So, we want to encourage her to make as much noise as she wants, because that will help."

"Oh," Benny said. "Should we make noise, too?"

Daisy had gone limp in his arms while he was speaking, but he heard her chuckle at that.

"No," Kellan said. "But I can use your help with something. It's important doctor work, though."

"Okay," Benny said, his little face going dead serious.

"I need you to help me put the comforter on Daisy's bed," Kellan told him. "And then I need you to grab my medical bag out of the office."

"Okay," Benny said.

They moved slowly into the bedroom, and Kellan whipped off the quilt and replaced it with his brand-new down comforter, feeling grateful that he had something warm and soft for her.

"Do you know where I keep my bag?" he asked Benny.

Benny nodded up and down.

"Okay, go get it," he told him. "We're counting on you."

"It will take him less than a minute," he told Daisy. "I'm going to take your coat off you now. Tell me if another contraction is coming so we can get you lying down."

By the time her coat was off, Benny was back with the bag.

"Great job," Kellan told him.

"Now what?" Benny asked.

"We need towels and blankets," Kellan told him. "But they have to be clean, so just the ones in the linen closet and in the trunk in my room. Do you think you could gather those carefully?"

"Yes, Dad," Benny said.

"Bring them one or two at a time, so you don't drop any," Kellan told him. "We need every single one, so it will probably take you a while, but that's okay. Put them on the dining room table. We'll be so glad to have them when the baby comes. We'll need to clean her off and bundle her up nice and warm on a cold night like tonight."

"Yes, Dad, I'll do it," Benny told him.

"When you finish up, I want you to fix yourself a healthy snack," Kellan told him. "Then you can turn on the television and watch as much as you want."

"I can?" Benny's eyes were big as saucers.

"You want to wait up and meet the baby, don't you?" Kellan asked.

Daisy began to moan again.

"Blankets and towels," Benny said worriedly.

"Yes," Kellan told him. "This is going exactly the way it's supposed to."

Benny dashed away.

Kellan said a silent prayer of thanks that the boy was well-behaved and helpful.

When her contraction was finished, he kept his arms around Daisy.

"The next thing I need you to do is remove all the clothing from the bottom half of your body," he told her. "I'll help you if it's okay. And then you can put the fluffy blanket on your lap to stay warm."

She nodded weakly and he breathed a sigh of relief.

He had been afraid she might feel shy or embarrassed, but she saw him as a doctor right now. And that made all the difference.

He got her squared away with the blanket on her lap before the next contraction hit.

The comforting sound of Benny going up and down the stairs told him that his son was doing just as he had been told.

"It's-it's going to hurt," Daisy whimpered, looking up at him bravely. "Isn't it?"

"Yes," he told her honestly, sitting on the chair beside the bed. "But you're a tough person, and I know you can do it. Now, how long have you been having contractions?"

He could see her focus change from fear to figuring out the timeline, and he felt reassured himself as they went through the usual questions a doctor asked an expecting mother before a birth.

32

DAISY

Daisy was lost in an ocean of pain, Kellan's strong, calm voice the only thing anchoring her to the world.

"One more good push," he told her. "And then you can meet your daughter."

She called on a strength she didn't know she had.

One moment there was only a burning agony that had no beginning or end.

And the next, relief.

Followed by the sweet, sweet sound of her furious daughter, screaming with indignation at being born.

"Baby," she sighed, tears streaming down her face.

"She's beautiful," Kellan breathed.

Then he was handing her a wrinkly pink bundle of perfection, wrapped up snugly in one of Sadie Wilkinson's soft shawls that had been left behind in the closet.

"Hello," Daisy whispered to her daughter.

The little one quieted, and blinked up at her with wondering eyes.

The love she felt was so intense that it was almost

painful. She knew to her bones she would do everything in her power to protect her daughter, and ensure that her life was filled with happiness.

"Ten fingers, ten toes," Kellan told her quietly. "She's healthy and perfect."

After the excitement she had caused coming into the world, the little one appeared to be tuckered out. She snuggled into her mother's arms and closed her eyes.

"I'll go get some more blankets and towels," Kellan said.

He was back in a heartbeat, cleaning her up expertly and then replacing the blankets so that she and the baby were nestled in a warm, dry bed.

"Kellan," she said. "I don't know how to thank you..."

"This was a privilege, Daisy," he told her, his eyes glistening.

"You're going to make me cry," she scolded him half-heartedly. "And then she'll cry."

He smiled at that, and the warmth in his eyes made her feel like he had hugged her and spun her around in his arms.

"Is it okay to let Benny come say hello?" he asked.

"Of course," Daisy told him.

For a moment she was cocooned with her daughter, still breathless and wrung out from their shared adventure.

Though she was early, the baby had been breech. Kellan had been forced to take desperate measures to get her turned around. It had been anything but an easy birth.

Daisy didn't like to think about what might have happened if she hadn't made it the two blocks in the snow to Kellan.

"We're so lucky," she murmured to her daughter, stroking a silken cheek gently with her fingertip.

"Daisy," Benny whispered excitedly as he darted in. "Your baby is here."

"I'm so glad that you and your dad were here to help us," Daisy told him.

Benny was carrying a nice fuzzy blanket in his arms. He held it out to her, and she wrapped it around the baby and herself.

"Oh, that's so nice and warm," she said with a smile. "I think she likes it."

Benny looked like he was going to explode with pride.

"Hi baby," Benny said softly, bending down. "What's your name?"

"You know, I had a couple of names picked out," Daisy said thoughtfully. "But I don't think any of them are right. I think I know just the name for this sweet girl. A name that honors the gift that you and your father, and all the nice people in this town gave to her and to me."

"What is it?" Benny asked, leaning in like she was going to tell him a secret.

"Hope," Daisy said simply.

She heard Kellan hiss in a breath.

"That's nice," Benny said. "You have a pretty name, Hope."

Daisy smiled down at the two small people who were so important in her life.

"Daisy," Benny said softly. "Can we tell my dad?"

"Can we tell him what?" she asked.

"About the money," he said, looking up at her with guilty eyes. "And about the Switch?"

"You didn't tell him already?" she asked, honestly surprised.

He shook his head, looking down at his feet.

"Benny Webb, you look at me," she told him fiercely.

"First of all, you are the most loyal friend I've ever had, and I do mean *ever*. Second of all, I should never have told you a secret without sharing it with your dad. I made a big, big mistake with that, and I'm sorry. You don't ever have to keep a secret from your grown-up, no matter who asks. Okay?"

He smiled then, and nodded hard.

"Why don't you go get ready for bed?" she asked him. "I'd like to tell your dad everything myself."

"Okay," Benny said. "I'm so happy about your baby."

"Me too," she said, shaking her head. "I just can't believe she's here."

Benny leaned in and she wrapped an arm around him.

He hugged her back gently and then dashed off, presumably to get ready for bed again.

"I can't believe he didn't tell you," she said.

"He seemed torn, so I didn't push. And you don't have to tell me either," he said. "At least not tonight. And not ever, if you don't want to."

"It's really pretty simple," Daisy told him as she studied her daughter's beautiful little face. "When Finn died in the mine, the company gave me a pay-out because of the faulty equipment. At first, I wanted to tear it to pieces. But I cashed the check instead, and I've been trying to get rid of the money ever since."

"What do you mean *get rid of* the money?" Kellan asked, his brow furrowed.

"After so much tragedy, I felt like the money was cursed," Daisy said. "I know that sounds silly, but I couldn't shake the feeling. And it felt like the only way to break the curse was to give all the money away without anyone knowing it was from me. It was a way for me to make something good out of all the terrible things that happened."

"*You're* the Trinity Falls Secret Santa," Kellan breathed, his eyes wide. "I can't believe it."

She had to laugh at his shocked expression.

"Daisy, I—I'm so sorry," he said suddenly. "Here I thought you had gotten tangled up in something bad, and instead, you were using your own money to do good all over town."

"It was a lot of money," she said. "I know it's not normal to carry that kind of cash around."

"I should have asked you," he said. "And that's all there is to it. But I'm glad you told me. And I'm definitely honored to be friends with the Trinity Falls Secret Santa."

"Well, I had a good run," Daisy laughed. "But I have a feeling this little lady's going to put a stop to my giving for a while. It's too bad. I was making a list of a whole bunch of stuff I wanted to give people for Christmas."

"Well, now that you have two elves instead of one, and one of those elves has a driver's license, maybe we can help you out," Kellan told her, with a smile. "If it ever stops snowing."

They both gazed out the window into the curtain of white.

"But for now, Benny and I will be glad to have you and little Hope to ourselves," Kellan said softly.

"I thought about what you said," she told him. "It feels like a lifetime ago, even though it was only this afternoon."

He gazed down at her intently, his blue eyes as brilliant as the ocean in summer.

"I care about you, too," she told him. "I did some soul-searching tonight. And I've realized that I'm more than where I come from, or the things that happened to me."

"Daisy," he said. "I hope I didn't—"

"You didn't," she assured him with a smile. "You never,

ever did. I'm ready to embrace my new life, and all the doors that are opening for Hope and me. And that includes yours."

The expression on his face was enough to have made everything she had gone through worth it. He looked at her like she was his whole world.

She smiled up at him, wondering if he could see the love in her eyes as easily as she could see it in his.

"Would it be okay if I scooted in next to you?" he asked.

She nodded.

Kellan sat beside her, wrapping an arm around her shoulder, and they looked out at the falling snow, as baby Hope slept on her chest.

There was so much to say, and at the same time, no need to say it. Everything was coming together. They had the rest of their lives to plan. For now, it was enough to share this moment of incredible peace.

A few minutes later, Benny slipped into the room, wearing his plaid flannel Christmas pajamas.

Kellan opened his arms and Benny climbed in, placing one of his little hands on Daisy's shoulder as he snuggled in.

A deep sense of satisfaction settled over her like a warm blanket. For the first time in a long time, she had no desire to keep moving. She really was right where she was supposed to be.

This is our family now, she realized happily as she drifted off to sleep. *This is home.*

33

DAISY

Daisy watched Kellan getting ready to load up the car the afternoon of Christmas day.

The serious, confident, older man she adored was nowhere to be found. Instead, she was watching an anxious new father who was clearly beside himself with worry. He checked and rechecked the diaper bag he had put together for her after walking over to the Mickelwaite place as soon as the snow stopped. Then he rearranged the home-made cookies he and Benny had prepared in their boxes to be brought over to his parents.

"I'm just going to take one last look at the car seat," he told her, pulling on his coat.

"You checked it twice already," she protested.

"Can't be too careful," he said. "Are you sure you're ready for this?"

He had called in a friend who was an OB to check on her this morning as soon as the roads cleared, and a neighbor who was a pediatrician had walked over to check on Hope.

Both of the Mullen girls were in great shape, thank goodness.

And though Daisy was a little nervous about spending the evening with Kellan's family, she knew the sooner she got over that hump, the easier everything would be.

Surely, no one would expect her to be especially vivacious with a brand-new newborn in her arms.

Once Kellan had checked the carseat again, and Benny had trotted downstairs with homemade cards for his grandparents, they all headed out to the driveway.

Kellan had shoveled early in the morning, so there was a clear path to the car. But the snow was high on either side, dazzling in the afternoon sunlight. Ice sparkled on the bare branches of the trees that formed a sort of tunnel over the street. The whole thing looked like a postcard of some winter wonderland.

"It's beautiful," Daisy said softly.

"When Hope gets bigger, I'll teach her to make snow angels," Benny said confidently.

"She will love making snow angels with you, Benny," Daisy told him.

Kellan strapped tiny Hope into her car seat with such care that it made Daisy's heart ache.

They drove slowly through Trinity Falls village, admiring the snowy vistas in silence. Before long, the town gave way to the main road, and then the land spread out around them into snow-covered farmland.

"Almost there, baby Hope," Benny whispered.

When they pulled up in front of the house, Daisy gasped. She'd never seen anything like it before.

"Oh, right," Kellan said. "This is Timber Run. I know it's unusual to see a contemporary house out here. My dad had it built for my mom when they got married, because she loves midcentury modern architecture."

"It's amazing," Daisy said.

"Benny, want to go see if Grandma left that thing on the porch for us?" Kellan asked.

Benny hopped out and ran up the stairs to the porch, grabbing something from the little table before he ran back down.

Kellan gave him a thumbs up, and then got baby Hope out of her carseat. She looked even tinier, cradled in Kellan's arms, and Daisy was lost for a moment in the vision of the two of them together.

Then Benny came running back, an excited look on his face.

"Everybody's looking at us through the window," he told his father.

"Well, I guess I'm over my stage fright, so we may as well do this in front of everyone," Kellan laughed.

Daisy looked between the two of them, wondering what was going on.

"Do you want to take her?" Kellan asked, referring to Hope.

"Yes," Daisy said, smiling as she took her bundled up daughter into her arms.

When she looked up, Kellan was on his knees with Benny standing beside him.

What was happening began to dawn on her, but she still couldn't believe it.

"Daisy, I love you," Kellan said simply. "And you make our household feel complete. Will you and Hope make Benny and me the happiest Webb boys on the planet, and agree to be a family with us?"

"Wait," Benny said with a huge grin. "What's this behind your ear?"

She smiled and watched with tears in her eyes as he reached behind her ear and pulled out something tiny and shimmering.

Benny handed it to his dad and stepped back, smiling.

"Daisy Mullen, will you marry me?" Kellan asked.

"Yes," she whispered.

Then he was slipping the ring over her finger, as someone in the house called to Benny.

"*She said yes,*" Benny was shouting happily as he ran off.

Daisy blinked down at the pretty little ring with the tiny diamond surrounded by intricate flowery swirls of gold.

"It was my great-aunt's," Kellan said gruffly. "You can choose another if you'd like. I didn't have a chance to shop with all the snow."

"I love it," she whispered. "And I love you."

He pulled her as close as the baby in her arms would allow, and his intense blue eyes met hers for a moment before he bent down to claim her mouth with his.

She knew his whole family was probably watching them out the window. But the moment his lips touched hers, she forgot all about them. She forgot all about everything.

There was only the heat of his mouth, the possessive way he held her, and the knowledge that this was forever.

At last, he pulled back, leaving her trembling.

"I don't want to stop," he told her, his voice husky with wanting. "I hope you don't want one of those weddings that needs to be planned a year in advance."

"Definitely not," she whispered.

"I just want to let you two know you have a house full of witnesses," a woman's voice called down cheerfully.

Kellan chuckled.

"Coming, Ma," he yelled back. "Ready for a night with a big, loud, noisy family?"

"Definitely," Daisy laughed. "I can't think of a better way to finish off our first Christmas together."

He took her hand and they headed for the house.

The crowd gathered round the doorway moved backward, letting them inside the most beautiful house Daisy had ever seen. The hardwood floors were gorgeous, but it was the massive Christmas tree, whose top practically scraped the high ceiling, that held Daisy's attention.

The tree was beautifully decorated with a mix of delicate lights and lumpy homemade ornaments, obviously crafted by kids over the years and beloved by their doting parents and grandparents.

"Welcome to the family," Kellan's mom cried, pulling Daisy into her arms but being very careful of the baby. "Merry Christmas."

"Thank you," Daisy said softly. "Merry Christmas."

Mr. Webb was standing by the stairs. He gave her a warm smile, a wink, and a little wave over his wife's shoulder.

"Goodness, you're as tiny as I am," Mrs. Webb cried, pulling back and having a good look at her. "I'll finally have someone to share clothes with."

Daisy laughed and felt more at home right away, even as Kellan's brothers Jared and Derek walked in, elbowing each other and laughing.

She had seen them around town, though they hadn't officially met.

"Leave it to Kellan to land a girl *and* a baby," Jared teased. "He's such an overachiever."

"Congratulations," Derek said with a big smile.

Before they could embrace there was a knock at the door.

"Brody," Mrs. Webb cried.

And then the door was open and cold air and guests were spilling in all over again.

Benny was super excited to see his cousins, Sam and Maddy.

And Brody was accompanied by a dark-haired girl who was smiling and blushing as Brody held out her hand to show his parents.

"*Oh, Brody,*" Mrs. Webb cried out. "You and Sarah are engaged?"

Kellan reached over and squeezed Daisy's hand.

"Amazing timing," she whispered to him.

When Mrs. Webb was finished fussing over Brody and his fiancée she turned to the others.

"Well, that's Brody, Lucy, and Kellan all accounted for," she said, pretending to wash her hands of her engaged children. "Now it's up to you boys, and Josh, of course."

She was eyeing Jared and Derek.

The two of them exchanged a look Daisy could only have described as terrified, much to the amusement of everyone else, who laughed uproariously at them.

"Maybe Josh will be next," Jared suggested.

"Yes, that seems fair," Derek added.

"He left town," Jared said. "He's got to take one for the team."

"You two are incorrigible," Mrs. Webb laughed. "Let's go have some supper."

"Gosh, Ma," Jared said, trailing after her. "I can't believe you just want to marry us off and get rid of us."

"I like grandchildren," Mrs. Webb teased, shrugging. "I want more."

"Your mother wants enough grandchildren to start her own marching band," Mr. Webb teased, his eyes twinkling. "And you know she always gets her way, boys. There's no point resisting."

Mrs. Webb stopped and put a kiss on her husband's cheek.

"You're a keeper, Simon Webb," she told him.

Kellan wrapped an arm around Daisy's shoulder as they followed the others into the kitchen.

The food smelled amazing, and she could hear Benny and his cousins laughing in the next room.

With Hope in her arms and Kellan beside her, Daisy couldn't imagine anyone had ever had a happier Christmas.

34

KELLAN

A few days after Christmas, Kellan stepped into his living room to find Daisy trying to put on a pair of snow boots.

"Where do you think you're going, Secret Santa?" he teased. "I thought you were going to let your elves handle this delivery."

It was a few days after Christmas, and although the roads were plowed, a lot of folks hadn't managed to clear their walks yet. But Daisy was clearly eager to deliver the small gifts and baked goods they had prepared for their neighbors.

"Would you judge me if I told you I sort of want to get out of the house for a few minutes?" she asked, an adorably worried look on her sweet face.

"Not at all," he had chuckled. "I'll tell you what. Why don't I take you over to the café to drink hot chocolate and catch up with Holly while Benny and I deliver the presents? That'll be more fun for you and Hope, and I won't have to worry about you slipping in the snow."

"Have I told you lately that you're the best fiancé ever?" she asked him.

"Every single day," he smiled.

"And I meant it every time," she told him with a wide smile.

After they all bundled up, he dropped her and Hope off safely at the window table of *Jolly Beans,* where she was already holding court by the time he paid for her breakfast.

Benny was wiggly with excitement the whole time to get back and deliver gifts. Once they got home, he went right to work. Kellan smiled as he watched the boy pile his sled high with packages.

"You know none of these are for us, right?" Kellan asked him.

"I like giving presents," Benny said, nodding. "Daisy showed me. It makes you feel *amazing.*"

"She's super smart, isn't she?" Kellan asked.

"She's a nurse," Benny said. "She knows how to make people feel better, just like you."

"She sure does," Kellan said, realizing that Daisy had more ways of making people feel better than he did. He used his training, but she used her whole heart. He and Benny were both learning a lot from her.

"You ready?" he asked.

"Very ready," Benny told him.

They headed out of the garage and into the beautiful sunny morning.

"The snow is still here," Benny said happily.

"That was a big one. It's going to take forever to melt," Kellan told him. "We might even get more snow on top of this snow."

"It will feel like Christmas forever," Benny laughed.

"I guess you're right," Kellan said.

They headed automatically to the house next door, where Benny ran up the front walk and knocked on the door. A moment later, it opened to reveal an elderly lady wearing a bright red Christmas sweater.

"Is that little Benny Webb?" she asked with a big smile.

"Hi, Mrs. Foster," Benny squeaked. "We have a present for you."

"My goodness, young man," Mrs. Foster beamed. "You stay there for one minute while I go find Mr. Foster. He'll want to say thank you."

Benny nodded and hopped up and down as Mrs. Foster disappeared into her house.

"Come get their present," Kellan called to him.

Benny ran down the walk again, found the Foster's present, and ran back up, just as both Fosters appeared in the doorway.

"Merry Christmas *late*," Benny sang out as he handed over the package, wrapped in pretty paper.

"Why thank you, young man," Mr. Foster said. "You know what this reminds me of?"

Benny shook his head.

"When your daddy was a little boy, he used to deliver the newspaper," Mr. Foster said fondly. "And he pulled a wagon full of papers, just like he's pulling a sled full of presents now."

Mr. Foster laughed, and Kellan joined in.

"Don't worry," he called to Mr. Foster. "I'm not collecting three dollars anymore."

Mr. Foster laughed even harder at that. His wife smiled and shook her head.

"We have to deliver more presents now," Benny told them.

"Of course, dear," Mrs. Foster said. "We'll see you soon.

And Mr. Foster and I will get in touch with your dad soon to schedule our check-up."

Kellan felt a jolt of joy at that. He worried about his neighbors in that big house at their age, and was glad they would be in touch on a professional basis so he could make sure they were in good health.

Benny bounced down the walkway to him and they kept walking.

"They want you to be their doctor," Benny said.

"I'm very grateful for that," Kellan told him. "It's an honor to be trusted."

Funnily enough, Daisy had helped with that, too.

He had been complaining that people in town only saw him as the paperboy.

And she had reminded him that the memories they had meant that they *knew* him, and they liked him. She was from one small town, and moving to another, so she knew that it was much easier to be remembered as part of the fabric of the town than to have to gain trust as a stranger.

If people here are thinking of you as the Webb boy with the paper route, instead of the kid that ran off to the city to work at some fancy hospital, then you're doing something right, she had declared.

He had just stared at her slack-jawed for a moment, wondering how something so obvious to her, and so clearly right, had never once occurred to him.

That shift in perspective had changed his whole approach, and the more he leaned into his identity as *Leticia Webb's boy, who used to deliver the paper*, the more he found people seemed to feel comfortable with him.

It was going to change everything—not just encouraging patients to visit, but also helping him gently point them in the direction of the preventative care they needed once they were there.

And somehow, he was going to convince Daisy to come back and work with him again, if she wanted to, once the baby was ready to accompany her to the office. Or, if she preferred to stay home with Hope, then maybe when the little one was at school.

He had another thought in mind too, if Daisy wanted to pursue it. Trinity Falls Community College had a nursing program, and if she wanted to get her RN one day, she could walk to classes. A good nurse was always in demand.

"What are you thinking about, Dad?" Benny asked, using the same words Kellan often used on him when he was daydreaming.

"I was just thinking about Daisy," Kellan told him honestly.

"She's going to be my mom," Benny said lightly.

"That's right," Kellan told him. "You're going to have *two* moms."

"And Daisy loves me," Benny said.

"She sure does," Kellan agreed.

"Just like she loves Hope," Benny said. But this time there was a question in his voice.

Kellan stopped in his tracks and bent down to look the boy in the eyes.

"*Exactly* like that," he told him. "I promise you."

Benny nodded with a solemn expression and headed off to the next house.

AN HOUR LATER, they had dropped off all the gifts, put the sled back in the garage, and walked up the street to *Jolly Beans*.

Kellan pushed open the door, and they stepped into the warmth and fragrance of the little coffee shop.

Sure enough, Daisy was still at the table, Hope sleeping on her chest, regaling her admirers with a story.

"I practically fell into his arms," she was saying. "I was so panicked, that I didn't know up from down. I just wanted to scream and spin around in circles."

"I'll bet," Holly said. The normally active waitress was just leaning against the wall with her tray propped on her hip, listening wide-eyed to Daisy's story.

"And Kellan just said, *Take a deep breath. I've got you,* in this very serious voice," Daisy said, sighing happily. "He had me relaxed inside of two minutes, and even Benny was running to get blankets and towels."

"That easy, huh?" Carol Beck asked her, shaking her head.

"Oh, not easy at all," Daisy laughed. "This little lady was breech, and Kellan had to turn her."

Some of her audience hissed in a breath.

"You didn't even have an epidural," Carol whispered.

"Again, I was super scared," Daisy said, shaking her head. "But Kellan was cool as ice, and he talked to me so gently that I was able to focus. His calm and expertise definitely got me through."

Some of the ladies nodded to each other.

"Before I knew, it Hope was in my arms," Daisy said happily. "And, well, of course every moment of that excitement was so worthwhile."

She pressed her lips to Hope's little head.

"There's nothing like your first," Mrs. Lennox said, smiling down at the baby.

"Well, Benny will always be my first," Daisy said with a fond smile. "I still can't believe I have a nice big family now."

There were approving murmurs, and the girl next to her put an arm around Daisy's shoulder.

But Kellan was glancing down at Benny, praying his boy had heard.

Benny was looking at Daisy like she hung the stars. Her words had healed a sadness in him that she hadn't even known about.

"Benny," she called out, just noticing that he was there.

Benny took off like a rocket, making his way through the thicket of townspeople to get his arms around his mama.

Daisy hugged him back, looking over the top of his head at Kellan.

"I was just bragging on you a little," she admitted. "I hope you don't mind."

"Of course not," he said. "You made me sound like Batman or something."

Everyone chuckled.

"You *were* like Batman, Dad," Benny said, letting go of Daisy to look up at him.

"You sure are my superhero," Daisy said, winking at him.

In that moment, for the first time since coming home to Trinity Falls, Kellan truly felt like he was right where he belonged, with his past and his future right here in front of him, filling his heart with inexpressible joy.

"Ready to go home?" Daisy asked him.

He nodded, and watched as she said goodbye to everyone, feeling like he would explode with happiness.

"What are you thinking about?" Daisy asked him as they walked out into the beauty of a snow-covered Trinity Falls together.

He stopped in his tracks.

"I'm thinking about how happy I am," he admitted. "And wondering what I ever did to deserve you three."

Benny hugged him tight.

Daisy stepped in, joining the hug.

He cupped her sweet face in his hand, wishing he could make her understand how blessed he knew he was with her here.

"I know you've done a lot of good for this town," he murmured to her, "but you saying yes to us was the best gift you gave all year."

She tilted her chin up to smile at him, and he bent to brush his lips against hers, reveling in her softness and wishing they weren't in the middle of Park Avenue so he could keep kissing her.

"I just can't get enough of you," he told her, pulling back to look into her eyes again.

"Good thing you're going to be stuck with me forever then," she teased, winking at him.

"Forever isn't long enough, as far as I'm concerned," he told her.

Then Benny spotted his cousins farther down the block, and with a nod from Kellan, he was laughing and taking off to join them.

Kellan took Daisy's hand and followed his joyful son into the sweetness of the everyday life they would be sharing together from now on.

***

Thanks for reading **Doctor's Secret Santa!**

Want to read Kellan and Daisy's **SPECIAL BONUS EPILOGUE?** Sign up for my newsletter here (or just enter your email if you're already signed up!):

https://www.clarapines.com/doctorbonus.html

About the next book:

Do you want to find out what happens when Miss Caroline, the sweet children's librarian, finds herself falling for a rough and tumble cowboy? Will she learn how to not judge a book by its cover, or will she miss out on a love that's long overdue?

Be sure to check out **Cowboy's Christmas Librarian**

https://www.clarapines.com/librarian.html

ABOUT THE AUTHOR

Clara Pines is a writer from Pennsylvania. She loves writing sweet romance, sipping peppermint tea with her handsome husband, and baking endless gingerbread cookies with her little helpers. A holiday lover through and through, Clara wishes it could be Christmas every day. You can almost always figure out where she has curled up to write by following the sound of the holiday music on her laptop!

Get all the latest info, and join Clara's mailing list at:

www.clarapines.com

Plus, you'll get the chance for sneak peeks of upcoming titles and other cool stuff!

Keep in touch...
www.clarapines.com
authorclarapines@gmail.com
Tiktok.com/authorclarapines

facebook.com/ClaraPinesAuthor
twitter.com/clarapines
instagram.com/authorclarapines

Made in United States
Orlando, FL
02 July 2024

48530413R00146